Stanislav, my stiletto in his hand, was shaking his head, blood pouring from his nose as I got to my feet.

"So," he said thickly. "You made one fatal error after all."

I circled warily around the bodies, keeping low so that I could spring out of the way if he suddenly lunged at me.

"What was that?" I shouted over the wind. "Not killing you earlier tonight when I had the chance?"

Stanislav laughed. "That's not it at all. You made the assumption that I worked for Yushenko. He made the same error."

"Who do you work for then?" I asked. "The CIA?"

Stanislav began moving in toward me, and I continued circling to the left, toward the opposite side of the pilot house.

"The man you call the Puppet Master," the big Russian said, and for a second that stopped me . . .

NICK CARTER IS IT!

FROM THE NICK CARTER
KILLMASTER SERIES

Dedicated to the men of the
Secret Services of the
United States of America

A Killmaster Spy Chiller

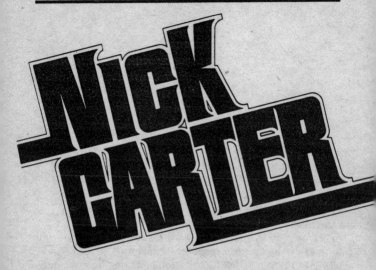

NICK CARTER

THE PUPPET MASTER

CHARTER
NEW YORK

A Division of Charter Communications Inc.
A GROSSET & DUNLAP COMPANY
51 Madison Avenue
New York, New York 10010

THE PUPPET
MASTER

Prologue

David Hawk, chief of AXE, the super secret action intelligence organization, left his office in the Amalgamated Press Building on Dupont Circle and climbed in the back seat of a plain gray sedan. Immediately the young Navy driver eased the car away from the curb and they headed north along Connecticut Avenue across the Taft Bridge.

Hawk was a well-built man in his early sixties. He had a thick shock of white hair, a broad, square face that seemed better suited for a scowl than a smile, and clenched in his teeth was an everpresent cigar.

It was a cold, stone-gray afternoon, and a biting north wind that had blown for the past two days seemed to have put everyone in Washington, D.C. on edge, including Hawk, who was at this moment a very worried man.

He had spent most of his life in service to his country, including the OSS during the War, the CIA when it was formed in the late forties, and finally the directorship of AXE—which had been created when the McCarthy witchhunts had effectively hamstrung many of the CIA's operations.

During those long years Hawk had observed the

missions he had authorized . . . sometimes from his office, which was called the Ivory Tower behind his back, and sometimes from the field.

He had sweated over hundreds of operations whose outcomes were doubtful from the very beginning. He had agonized over the occasional operation that had failed for one reason or another. And he had tried his damnedest to explain the precise function that AXE played in the security of the free world to eight incoming presidents.

During that time he had made some friends, but many more enemies. Hawk was the sort of person who never pulled his punches. He generally said what he thought when he thought it, and expected the same from the people around him.

As a result he was not a well-liked man. But he was respected. His decisions were looked upon by his staff almost as words of God. And every president so far, and the Joint Chiefs as well, held him in high regard.

On the other side of the coin, however, there were damn few men who had ever earned and then kept his respect. Among the few of them was Nick Carter, presently AXE's senior field man, who several years ago had earned the designation N3, Killmaster.

The driver turned off Connecticut Avenue onto Jones Bridge Road, breaking into Hawk's morose thoughts, and he looked up as they came through the back gate into the National Naval Medical Center compound and proceeded along a tree-lined lane.

Six months ago Hawk had signed the mission authorization forms which had sent Nick Carter to this place. And now as the car approached the parking lot behind the Psychological Research Building, he wondered if he hadn't signed Nick's death warrant as well.

Dr. T. Gillingham Wells, chief psychologist of the team that had been working on Nick for the past one hundred eighty days, was waiting by the elevator when Hawk came up. He was a huge, rotund man with a bright face and a billiard-ball-smooth head. He was not smiling this afternoon.

"Good afternoon, David," he said, his voice soft.

Hawk nodded and glanced down the corridor toward the security section where Nick had been housed all this time.

"Before you go in, there's something I have to say to you," Wells said, and Hawk turned to him.

"The conditioning took?"

"Not nearly well enough in my opinion," Wells said, a troubled expression crossing his features. "We need more time."

"How much more time?" Hawk asked sharply. He had a curious, unsettled feeling in his gut.

"I don't know. A few months, maybe longer."

"Maybe never?" Hawk asked.

"Dammit, David, Nick Carter is an almost impossible subject. He cooperates to a point, but then something inside of him stiffens up, and there's damned little we can do about it."

Hawk had to smile. "Will he break under pressure?"

Wells thought seriously about the question for a long moment, then shrugged. "I simply don't know. We've done our best with him, but I simply don't know what will happen to him if they subject him to torture or drugs. Everything we've done could fall apart."

"What do you mean by that?" Hawk asked.

Wells took Hawk by the arm and they headed slowly down the corridor. No one else was there at the moment.

"You must accept that an individual's personality, to a great degree, is nothing more than a sum total of his experiences. Of his memories, if you like."

"That's understandable," Hawk said carefully. Both he and Nick had reviewed the procedure six months ago, before the work had begun.

"In the past months we have altered Nick's memories . . . or at least we've tried. In most cases the changes are quite subtle, and subconscious. We're hoping that if he lets himself go when he's under pressure, he'll come up with an entirely new set of memories."

They stopped at the wire mesh gate that blocked the last hundred feet of corridor.

"We've tried to inject into his subconscious a wide range of memories and feelings about friends and associates who work with the CIA."

"So if he breaks or pretends to break, he'll convince them he worked for the Company."

"In theory," Wells said. "But I just don't know." He unlocked the gate and swung it open.

"I'll go in alone," Hawk said.

"Third door on the right. He's expecting you," Wells said. "But think about what I said, David. Nick isn't ready yet."

own devices. The thought was frightening.

I turned back to Dr. Wells. "I'll do my best," I said.

Wells managed a slight smile. "It's all we can ask," he said. "But it may not be enough in your case. We may not have the expertise."

At the one hundred fifty mark my muscles were screaming in protest. Sweat was pouring off me, but I continued. Down, hold a second; up, hold another second.

Kobelev. Code-named the Puppet Master because he was an expert at making people do what he wanted them to do, at pulling strings.

Seven months ago I had been involved in trying to stop one of his brilliantly planned operations, one that left more than a hundred innocent people dead, some of them horribly mutilated by radiation poisoning; that left relations between Israel and the U.S. badly strained; and that left the Japanese government screaming for restitution in the International Court in the Hague.

Kobelev had accomplished all that from his office at the KGB's headquarters on Dzerzhinsky Square in Moscow. All that from a position as chief of the Executive Action Department. With each promotion up the KGB's heirarchy Kobelev's operations became larger and much more dangerous.

"There will come a time," Hawk told me seven months ago when we first began to plan my mission, "when Kobelev will become so powerful that his operations could tip the delicate balance of world power."

"War," I had said softly. And I remember thinking at the time how amazing it was that one man, no matter how brilliant, how devious, could do such a thing. But then I thought of Hitler and what he had done in Europe.

At one hundred seventy-five my muscles were beginning to shiver spasmodically, and each push-up was agonizing, but I continued. Down, hold a second; up, hold another second.

During the four weeks before I was signed in here at the hospital, I had buried myself in AXE's archives in the basement of the Amalgamated Press Building on Dupont Circle, memorizing everything that we knew about Kobelev.

He was born in 1927 in a small fishing village outside Leningrad, of a poor family. His father had fought the Nazis, and was the chairman and chief political officer fo his village's party cell, so that in 1945 when the war in Europe had ended, the young Nikolai Fedor was given a place at Moscow State University, where he studied political science, earning his degree in 1949 at the age of twenty-two. He went to work immediately as a cipher clerk for the Ministry of State Security, one of the forerunners of the present day KGB.

From there Kobelev rose quickly through the ranks, although there weren't too many details in our files for this period of his life. But in 1954, when the KGB was finally formed, he emerged at the tender age of twenty-seven as a full-fledged case officer in Department S, and had the job of spying from Soviet embassies in the world's capitals.

It was during this period, according to our files, that Kobelev's true colors began to emerge. Wherever the man surfaced . . . Lisbon in the mid-fifties, Berlin in the early sixties, Buenos Aires in the late sixties and early seventies . . . the free world's influence was diminished. American and British agents were killed; ships, trains and aircraft were sabotaged; military installations compromised; and codes broken. Wherever Kobelev went, he left behind a trail of death and destruction that grew in size as he grew in experience.

By 1975, according to our files, no less than eight attempts to assassinate him had been made by us and the British, not one of them even coming close. But that year Kobelev dropped out of sight until he resurfaced a couple of years ago and suddenly became the chief of Department V . . . the Executive Action branch of the KGB.

At one hundred ninety my heart was pounding nearly out of my chest, each breath sending sharp, hot stabs of pain throughout my body, and my arms seemed like little more than dead slabs of useless meat. Yet I continued. Down, hold a second; up, hold another second.

"One ninety-six," I gasped, and I started down again.

"One ninety-seven," someone said from behind me as I came up, held a second, and started down again.

I heard the voice behind me as if it was coming from a very great distance, and I knew I should recognize it, but I was intent on what I was doing. I had set a goal for myself and nothing was going to stop me from reaching it.

"One ninety-eight," the voice came to me as I reached the top and started down.

This simple little exercise would not beat me, I thought, nor would Kobelev. Our files showed that the man was heavily guarded at all times. In addition he was in outstanding physical condition, was an expert pistol shot, had taken martial arts training since he was a young man, and it was said he was as strong as a bull.

At one hundred ninety-nine the last push-up seemed like an insurmountable hurdle, but at the bottom, my chin brushing the floor, holding there a full second, a new resolve coursed through me, I could do two hundred fifty if I had to. This last one was nothing.

Somehow I was coming up, my arms straightening, every muscle screaming, and the voice behind me said, "Two hundred," just as I reached the top, held one full second, and then let myself go, slipping gratefully to the floor where I closed my eyes as I caught my breath.

"Impressive." The voice I now recognized as Hawk's came to me through my haze, and I looked up as he crossed the room and sat down on the edge of the table.

I lay where I was for a few moments longer, feeling my strength rapidly returning, and finally I got up, went across the room to my bed, laid the exercise jacket aside and grabbed a towel to wipe the sweat from my face and neck.

"Good afternoon, sir," I said. "Did Dr. Wells break the news to you?"

Hawk seemed to be studying me, but he nodded. "He doesn't think you're ready yet. He wants more time."

I shook my head. "There's no guarantee that I'll be any further along in six months than I am right now," I said. My muscles ached, but it was a good ache. I wasn't stiffening up. I was in better physical condition now than I had ever been.

"Even if I didn't agree, Nick, it would be a moot

point. We don't have the time."

Hawk was worried. I could see it in his eyes. And when he was concerned, it meant something very big was happening, or was about to happen.

"What has he done now?" I asked.

Hawk turned and glanced out the window, across the medical compound. "It's not Kobelev himself, it's the Soviet Presidium," he said, and he turned back.

"Sir?"

"They meet in fourteen days. Kobelev's name is on the agenda, according to our sources."

"A promotion?" I asked.

Hawk nodded, but said nothing.

"My God, if Kobelev becomes head of the First Chief Directorate, there's no telling what he'll manage to do."

"It's bigger than that," Hawk said, definite lines of worry around his eyes and mouth. "The CIA managed to decode a batch of A-channel intergovernmental dispatches, and they were passed on to us. Kobelev's name will be coming up for promotion as chairman of the entire KGB."

I was stunned, and it must have shown on my face.

"We knew it was coming sooner or later, but not quite this soon."

"What are his chances?" I asked, recovering somewhat from my surprise.

"Very good, I expect. They're all afraid of him. Already he's so powerful no one in the Soviet Union wants to cross him."

"Then I'll have to go now. It'll have to be done within fourteen days."

"You can't fail, Nick," Hawk said with emotion.

"And yet I have doubts about your chances for success."

I had been on many so-called "impossible" assignments before, but I was a pragmatic man. I've never deluded myself into believing in dreams. This time I shared Hawk's doubts. My chances for success were very small. Yet I had no other choice. Kobelev had to be stopped.

Hawk glanced at his watch. "It's just four-thirty. It'll be dark in a couple of hours," he said, and he looked up at me. He had carried a cheap plastic briefcase in with him, and had laid it on the table. "Your things are in here," he said tapping it with a blunt, nicotine-stained finger. "Weapons, money, identification, and the CIA case files and operational notes you made before you came here."

"I'll leave tonight," I said.

"Seven o'clock," Hawk said. "Dr. Wells will call the Bethesda Police and tell them you've escaped. Meanwhile I'll inform the FBI, and we'll quietly begin to take Washington apart looking for you."

"Not too quietly," I said in an attempt at humor that failed.

"The opposition will know we're looking for you, but whether they'll swallow it or not is another question."

Everything was set. We had worked out most of the details months ago, and there was nothing left now other than action. Kobelev was brilliant, and if he even so much as expected I wasn't what I claimed to be, I would be killed without hesitation.

"How about Moscow?" I asked.

"Brad Hollinger is our man there in the news service office. Your code word is *marionette* if you're in trouble. He'll get you to the embassy and from there it will be in the hands of the diplomats."

If it went that far it would mean I had failed, I thought. And even if I did manage to reach Hollinger it would be one hell of a trick actually getting me into our embassy, which was heavily guarded twenty-four hours a day by Soviet troops.

That was nothing, however, compared to my mission. The first step would be for me to defect to the Soviet Union, and convince them I was what I claimed to be: A high-ranking, but disgruntled CIA case officer.

The second step was for me to spout Kobelev's name whenever and wherever I could. I was to ask not only for political asylum, but I was to demand an audience with Kobelev.

When—or if—I got that far I was to gain the man's confidence in any way possible. That was going to be the most delicate maneuver in the mission.

"At that point," Hawk had told me months ago, "Kobelev will almost certainly send you out of the Soviet Union on some kind of a test mission."

He had come downstairs into Archives, where I was studying the Russian's files. No one was in earshot, nor were there any tape recorders running as there always were up in Hawk's office.

"I don't know if I'd be able to do anything like that," I said. "I mean if Kobelev sends me out to blow up a passenger aircraft, or assassinate the Prime Minister of England, or something like that, I just couldn't go along with it."

"Yes you could, and you will. It'll be up to us to stop you."

I was suddenly very uncomfortable. "A lot of good people could be killed."

After a long silence Hawk said, "It's possible. But that's my worry. You have a job to do."

Kobelev, from what we knew about his movements within the Soviet Union, had an apartment in Moscow on Kutzovsky Prospekt, but most of his time was divided between his office at KGB headquarters on Dzerzhinsky Square and his palatial dacha twenty-seven miles outside of Moscow.

The man was married and had a twenty-two-year-old daughter who lived with him. The family almost always remained at the dacha, however. Very rarely had they ever been seen in Moscow.

Those people in Kobelev's favor were invited from time to time to spend a weekend at his dacha in the countryside. It would be up to me to somehow ingratiate myself with the man, so that I too would be invited out there.

When the time was right, I was to kill him in such a fashion that his body would not be discovered for hours . . . days if possible . . . allowing me enough time to either escape the country across the Finnish border (I had done that once before), or run for Hollinger and our embassy in Moscow.

All those things ran through my mind now as I stood across the room from Hawk, who was still seated on the edge of the table in front of the window.

"It all hinges on whether or not they believe you're a disgruntled CIA case officer," Hawk said almost as if he had read my thoughts. "If they so much as suspect for a moment that you're anything else, they'll kill you."

"I know," I said. I wrapped the towel around my neck.

"Dr. Wells' car is outside in the back parking lot. The keys will be in the ignition. At seven o'clock he's going to call the police to report you missing, and to report his car stolen."

I'd have to be long-gone from the doctor's car by then, before seven. This mission was going to be tricky enough without me being forced into a confrontation with the local police.

I nodded.

"Any last questions?" Hawk asked.

"No."

"Good luck then, Nick," he said standing up.

"Thank you, sir. And thank Dr. Wells for me."

Hawk smiled. "You can thank him yourself when you get back."

It was a couple of minutes after five by the time Hawk had left. I had taken a shower and gotten dressed. The briefcase contained a 9mm Luger, my stiletto in its chamois sheath, a well-used CIA plastic identification card with my photograph and thumb print, five hundred dollars in small denominations, and several fat file-folders containing my notes on the CIA. It was information I was authorized to pass on to the Russians. All of it was genuine, and some of it would do us real harm.

But, as Hawk had explained it to me, it was nothing more than a trade-off. We were willing to trade this information in order to give me a chance to get at Kobelev. He was the real prize.

The Luger was the same model gun I've always used, but the serial number on this one had been left intact. Traceable with some difficulty, no doubt, back to the CIA.

I pocketed the ID card and money, strapped on

my weapons, and pulled on my jacket. Before I went to the door I looked around the room that had been home for the past six months, feeling absolutely no regret about leaving the safety of this place. In fact I was glad to be doing something again.

Although I don't especially like long odds against me, this mission was of supreme importance. If Kobelev were allowed to take over the entire KGB, we would be at war with the Soviet Union within a year . . . perhaps less.

The corridor was deserted and the gate in the wire mesh barrier had been left ajar for me by Hawk. I hurried down the hall and let myself out of the security section, closing and locking the gate behind me.

At the end of the corridor I took the stairs down two at a time, emerging from the back door a couple of minutes later, the briefcase tucked under my arm.

The shift change at the hospital had come and gone while Hawk and I were talking, and the back parking lot was less than half full now with the night crew's cars.

I nonchalantly strolled across the driveway to the front row of cars parked in their reserved slots, and slipped behind the wheel of Dr. Wells' late-model Chrysler.

The keys were in the ignition as Hawk said they would be, and when I had the car started and backed out of its parking spot, I glanced up at the windows on the fourth floor of the Psychological Research Building. Dr. Wells was at his window looking down at me, and when our eyes met he waved, and then turned away.

Like Hawk, I suspect, Dr. Wells was certain he would never see me alive again, and it gave me a strange feeling in the pit of my stomach to know that at least two people were sure I was going to my death.

I put the car in gear and headed out of the parking lot along the back road and out the rear gate onto Jones Bridge Road.

In something under two hours Wells would be calling the police, but it would take the authorities at least an hour to get organized before they would begin checking the railroad and bus depots, the airport and the car rental agencies in town. By then I would be long gone.

Hawk's inquiries with the FBI later this evening would help somewhat by keeping the main thrust of the search centered in the Washington area.

Meanwhile I would be in New York City. Sooner or later, however, they would find Dr. Wells' car where I was going to park it, on a ramp here in town, and they would come across the Hertz rental agency where they would find out that I had rented a car for a trip to Chicago.

That might throw them for a day or two, but again, sooner or later the Hertz car would be found in New York. By then I hoped to be out of the country. On my way to Kobelev.

Two

The weather was blustery, the wind driving long streaks of cold rain into my face as I stumbled down East Forty-second Street toward First Avenue.

I had purchased a suit of threadbare clothes along with a slouch hat from a Salvation Army store earlier that day. At a hobby shop I had bought a couple of pieces of cork which I had burned and used to darken my face as if I hadn't shaved in several days. And at another shop I had picked up a cane.

It wasn't much of a disguise, but it was enough for the moment until the search for me intensified here in New York. The story of an escaped murderer from the Bethesda Naval Hospital had made the front pages in the Washington paper this morning, but only a brief mention of it appeared in the back pages of the New York *Times*.

At the busy intersection I waited until the light changed and then limped across First Avenue and the half a block to the United Nations' building's main gate.

It was just six o'clock and a stream of people were leaving the building, some of them in their personal cars, some of them by limousine, many on foot, and a number racing for the dozen or so cabs that had pulled up.

Among the more than two hundred Soviet nationals working for the United Nations Secretariat in New York City, at least two dozen were known or suspected KGB agents.

And among those two dozen, my target for first contact was Oleg Dmitrevich Yushenko, who worked for the Soviet delegation. But I had to first make sure that Yushenko was in New York this week. He often traveled out of the country, and at least once a month made a trip down to Washington to the Soviet Embassy.

He was a short, balding man who was said to have a huge collection of Botany 500 suits which he kept in his apartment on Park Avenue. His wife and two children had remained in Moscow when he was assigned to the U.N. eighteen months ago, but during his stay here he was seldom if ever lonely for female company.

The man was what we called a "front." Because of his flamboyant behavior the Soviets expected we would watch him very closely, which we had. Their theory was that if we were preoccupied with Yushenko, we might not notice what some of their other people were doing.

A couple of months ago the watchdogs had been very quietly taken off Yushenko at Hawk's suggestion, and were instead concentrating on two other men in the Soviet delegation who had been working to convert a Navy commander at our submarine base at New London.

Yushenko was, therefore, a free agent at the moment, the most logical one for me to contact.

Hawk had made certain that the shift in surveillance teams was done in a very routine way. It was something that was done from time to time, and hopefully would create no suspicion.

We were sure the Soviets would immediately spot the shift, and the risk we were taking was that Yushenko would be immediately ordered into a some kind of project that would take him away from New York.

The crowd from the building had grown by the time I reached the gate, and as I stepped aside for a group of young Oriental secretaries, I spotted my man less than ten feet away heading for one of the cabs.

I lurched quickly to the left, and in half a dozen steps had come between him and the cab he had been heading for.

He glanced at me with annoyance, and started to step aside when I grabbed his left arm at the elbow.

"Greetings, Oleg Dmitrevich," I said softly.

No one was paying us any attention, but his eyes went wide and he looked behind me as if he suspected someone were watching. "How do you know my name?" he said.

With my left hand I reached in my coat pocket and withdrew a scrap of paper on which I jotted down several of the index numbers of the CIA case files I had brought with me, and handed it to him.

"What's this?" he said trying to step back away from me. The people streaming by effectively hid us from the view of the guards near the gate, but Yushenko looked that way, as if he were about to shout for help.

"Noon tomorrow at Washington Square Park in the Village. I'll bring the files with me," I said urgently. "Come alone."

I let go of his arm, turned around, and headed back the way I had come, putting as much distance as I could between myself and the startled KGB agent before he recovered his poise and reacted with some foolish move.

There was little doubt in my mind that if Yushenko calmed down sufficiently, and studied the scrap of paper I had given him, he would recognize the numbers and references for what they were.

If he showed up tomorrow, he wouldn't come alone of course. He'd have a backup crew. At least two men, possibly more. It would be a dangerous point for all of us. Yushenko would be nervous, his guards possibly trigger happy, and I would have to play my own part . . . the disgruntled CIA agent on the run, ready to jump at the slightest sign of trouble.

At the corner I crossed with the light and on the other side I glanced back. Yushenko was no longer there. But whether he had gone back inside, or had taken a cab, I had no way of knowing. I had made the first move, the next step was his.

I walked up to Second Avenue and I caught a bus to the East Village, where I walked the last few blocks to the shabby rooming house I was staying at.

"No cookin' in your room, no noise after ten at night, and no broads. Those are the only rules," the old man who ran the place had told me last night when I checked in. I paid two weeks rent in advance.

"Can't cook, don't snore, and got no use for broads anyway," I told him as I paid the money. I pulled a pint bottle of Old Crow from my jacket pocket, unscrewed the cap, took a deep drink, and offered him the bottle.

"Don't mind if I do," he said, and he drank nearly half of it before he handed it back. "We'll get along just fine, you and me," he said. "Just fine."

"Sure," I said laughing. I took another drink from the bottle and handed it back to him again. "Finish it," I said. "More where that came from."

When he finished the bottle, he patted me on the shoulder. I had gone directly up to my tiny room on the top floor and slept lightly. I went out at ten in the morning to check the Hertz rental car where I had parked it in a lot down near the Battery. It was still there and as far as I could see had not been spotted because there were no stakeouts on it yet.

I had spent most of the rest of the day in my room, going out finally around five to make that first contact with Yushenko. Now, wet and cold from the rain, I trampled into the front hall of the rooming house in time to meet the manager coming down the stairs. He had a guilty look on his face that deepened when he spotted me at the door. I knew damned well he had been in my room.

"Looking for something?" I asked, and he flinched.

"I . . . " he stammered, and he looked over his shoulder back up the dark stairway. "I was just . . . looking for you," he said. "That's it. I was looking for you. Thought maybe you'd like to come down and have a drink with me."

"No thanks," I starting up the stairs. He shrank

back away from me. "I'm tired. Going to bed."

"Sure," the man said. "You look kinda wore out."

I continued up the stairs, but at the first floor landing I stopped and listened for sounds from below. I could hear the manager muttering something to himself as he went to his room, then the door opened and closed, and the building was quiet.

Moving on the balls of my feet so as to make no noise, I hurried back down to the first floor and along the dark, narrow corridor to his room where I put my ear to the door.

At first I could hear nothing, but then the sound of a telephone dial whirring was distinct. A few moments later I could hear him talking.

"This is Sam. There was nothing up there."

It couldn't be the opposition, not this quickly, nor did I think he had telephoned the police.

"I'm telling you I looked everywhere. All that's up there are the clothes he came in with last night, a couple of bottles of booze, and a couple of deli sandwiches. No money. Nothing."

The clothes I had been wearing last night, when I had checked in, had been nothing special. Evidently, however, they had been just a little too fine for this neighborhood. I had paid too much rent in advance, and I had been too free with the booze as well. The old man and his friend were figuring me either for a fall guy, or someone on the run. Either way, if they lifted whatever cash I had, they figured I'd never call the cops.

"I think he's suspicious," the manager was saying. "He just came in as I was coming down the stairs."

I had to smile. They were a couple of small-time thieves. But they could cause me trouble unless I dealt with them immediately. I didn't want them getting in the way of the Soviets. If they did, someone would definitely get hurt.

I hurried noiselessly back down the corridor and up again to the first floor landing where I waited for a full two minutes before I started down, swearing loudly and thumping my fist on the wall.

As I rounded the corner on the first floor the manager was coming out of his room. When he saw me he turned a couple of shades of white and started to back away.

"You, goddammit," I shouted. I raced down the corridor and caught him by the front of his shirt before he could get all the way into his room and close the door.

"What's going on?" he stammered.

"Someone was in my room. Swiped my two hundred bucks I had hidden up in the light fixture. You were up there!"

The man was shaking his head, his eyes wide, his jaw working. "No . . ." he said. "I swear it. I didn't take your money."

I made as if I was going to hit him but then decided against it as I pulled him a little closer to me. "I want my money back. And I want it back quick."

"How do I know you had that kind of money?" the manager stammered in desperation.

I looked beyond him into his apartment. "The hell with it," I said, and I pushed him aside and went into the room to the phone. "I'll just call the cops. They can come down here and roust everyone out. We'll find my money."

"No!" the man shouted. "No . . . that's not necessary. We'll . . . I'll find your money for you. Don't worry. You'll get it back."

"How?" I snapped.

"I'll figure it out. I'll ask around. Someone will know something. Give me a couple of days. I'll get it back for you. Promise."

I seemed to think about it for a moment.

"I don't want no trouble in my place. That's all. Give me a couple of days."

I nodded finally. "See that you do. Forty-eight hours. And if I catch anyone near my room I'll call the cops right away."

I left his room and headed back upstairs, this time to get some sleep. My threat would keep them off my back and out of the way for a couple of days, plenty of time, I hoped, for me to finish my business here in New York.

I cleaned up in the bathroom down the hall from my room, then lay down on top of my bedcovers and closed my eyes. It took a long time for sleep to finally come, and as it finally did I had several disturbing images. One of them was a man whose name I somehow knew was Bob McKibbens, chief of Missions and Controls down at Langley. I could see his house in Alexandria very clearly. Only a part of me was still aware that I knew no such man.

By noon the day had become a carbon copy of yesterday with an icy rain that threatened to turn to snow at any moment, and a cold wind that seemed to be funneled down Fifth Avenue right into my face every time I peered around the edge of the Washington Arch.

On a warm, dry day there would be dozens of people in the park, some of them at the south end playing chess on the cement tables, others hawking used books or ties or pretzels, but today there was no one here.

I had shown up around eleven o'clock and had made a couple of cautious circuits around the square, but had been unable to spot anyone. The few cars parked on the side streets were empty, and as far as I could tell there were no stakeouts on any of the roofs.

Finally, a few minutes before noon, I had crossed the park, and took up position near the arch itself, to wait. If Yushenko wasn't going to take the bait, I was going to have to go to him, probably tonight at his apartment. That would be an exceedingly dangerous move, and one that could involve me with the New York City Police Department. Almost all the apartment buildings in Yushenko's neighborhood were guarded by security people.

I had brought two of the case files with me, stuffed under my belt beneath my coat. The others I had left in the briefcase I had hidden in one of the ventilator shafts on the roof of the rooming house.

Delicately, Hawk had told me, "If you come at them too strong they'll probably spook and stay clear of you."

But this was already the second day. In twelve days the Soviet Presidium would meet and consider Kobelev's promotion. If it came he would immediately be placed under a very strong independent surveillance and physical guard. Standard procedure for men of such high rank.

I was about to reach for a cigarette when a tan, four-door Chevrolet came down Fifth Avenue and turned west on Waverly Place. Besides the driver there was another man in the front seat and at least two in the back.

The car slowed down at the corner of Mac-Dougal, the front door on the passenger side came open, and a man got out. A moment later the car slowly moved south, and at the corner of East Fourth Street, it stopped again. This time one of the men in the back seat got out and the car turned up East Fourth to University Avenue where the second man in the back got out.

The car sped up then, disappearing down University Avenue toward the Washington Mews half a block away.

As if on signal, the three men who had gotten out of the car all started toward me, slowly, as if they were merely out for an afternoon's walk despite the weather.

Even from where I stood I could tell that none of them was Yushenko. They were all too big. Either he'd sent them here to make the rendezvous, exposing himself to no risk, or had been the one driving.

But I was a spooked agent on the run. Yushenko was the contact I had picked, and no one else would do.

I ducked back around the arch so that I was out of sight of the three men heading my way, and pulled out the Luger. I snapped the safety off and levered a round into the firing chamber.

A minute and a half later the closest of the three men came around the corner in a dead run, nearly falling all over himself trying to stop when he realized I was holding a gun on him.

"Call your partners off!" I snapped. "Now, or you're a dead man."

For an instant the big Russian hesitated, trying to decide what to do, but he was a professional and he realized that his life probably depended upon very quick action.

"Mikhail . . . Georgi! Stop! He has a weapon," he shouted.

For several moments we both waited, frozen into position. I had already decided that if either of the other two came around the arch, I would shoot this man. Three to one odds were difficult. Two to one I could handle.

"Are you all right?" One of the others called out. It sounded as if he was less than twenty feet away.

I nodded my head.

"Yes," the man I was holding the gun on said. "But he has a weapon. Do not come any closer."

"Where's Yushenko?" I asked.

"I don't know a Yushenko," he said, his Soviet accent heavy.

"Let me see your KGB identification card then," I snapped.

The man hesitated and I raised the Luger so that it was pointing directly at his head. "I want to see your identification, Comrade. Standard issue. U.N. Trade Delegation."

"Yushenko sent us," he said very softly.

"That's better," I said. I reached inside my coat and withdrew the two files I had brought with me, and carefully handed them to the man.

"There are nine others," I said. "I will personally give them to Yushenko here, tonight at midnight. He must come alone."

"You are wanted by the FBI for murder," the

agent said. Yushenko must have recognized me, and had done his homework.

I nodded, although I knew he was stalling for time. "That's right, so another murder won't mean much to me."

"What do you want?"

"Yushenko," I said harshly. "Here at midnight. I'll give him the other files."

"He won't come here alone. It's a trap."

I laughed. "You can tell Yushenko that he is to arrange transportation out of the country for me. I want to defect."

"We don't take common murderers," the man said disdainfully.

Again I laughed. "Yushenko will see from the files that I was a Clandestine Operations case officer with the Company. I have a lot of information he could use."

The man's eyes narrowed, and he was about to say something else, but I cut him off.

"No more talk. I want Yushenko here tonight at midnight. Alone. Tell him that I want to work for Kobelev."

The man reacted as if I had kicked him below the belt, but I didn't give him time for any other reaction.

"Tell your people to go across the street now, and head for your car," I said.

The man looked at the files he held in his right hand, then back up at me. "Mikhail . . . Georgi . . . go back to the car. Immediately," he called out.

There was nothing for a moment, and then my man shouted something about "extreme importance," in rapid-fire Russian, but I couldn't catch all of it.

Again we waited, but still there was no answer. The Russian was about to shout again when one of the men came into view across the street near the University Avenue intersection. A few seconds later the other appeared and together the two of them went around the corner.

"Now get out of here," I said stepping aside and motioning him away with the Luger. "And whatever you do, be careful with those files, they're important."

The man nodded, stared at me a moment longer, a new respect dancing in his eyes since my mention of Kobelev's name. Then he turned and walked rapidly away from the arch, crossed the street, went around the corner at University Avenue.

My bait had been taken, but whether or not Yushenko would risk meeting me here tonight was another question. I had not given the man enough time to check with his superiors in Moscow, so if he accepted my demands he would be acting on his own.

I wanted to keep them all off balance, at least for the moment—until my name could come to the attention of Kobelev himself.

After a full five minutes I was satisfied that Yushenko's goons were not going to double back on me. I holstered the Luger and headed out of the park in the general direction of my rooming house.

I would bring the rest of the files with me to the meeting with Yushenko to prove I was legitimate, and then I would promise much more information if I was allowed to defect.

There was a very good chance that as long as I continued to cooperate with them I would never undergo anything but the mildest of interrogations under drugs. But it would be up to me to at least suggest such methods in order to convince Kobelev of my sincerity.

That, along with Hawk's prediction that I would be sent out of the country on some sort of test mission, would hopefully win the man's confidence in me. Or at least enough of his confidence so that I could get close enough to him to accomplish the assassination and then make my escape.

As I walked I couldn't help but think of other missions I had been on. Other jobs in which the odds had been stacked pretty heavily against me. In one way or another I always managed to survive. Not always in style. And sometimes with a fairly hefty dose of luck. But from the beginning this operation had had the feel of a nightmare; a nightmare which I was compelled to see through to the end.

It took me a full hour to make it back to the street on which my rooming house was located, and as I turned the corner I looked up in time to see two men in white loading a body on a stretcher into the back of an ambulance.

There were three police cars, their red lights flashing, parked in front of the building, and a small crowd of people had gathered across the street.

I turned and started back around the corner when a blue Ford with no markings roared past me, skidded to a halt in the middle of the street, and two men who were obviously plainclothes of-

ficers jumped out. They spoke with several of the
uniformed cops, and a few minutes later went inside.

But I hadn't been paying much attention to
them. Instead my eyes were riveted on the roof,
where a uniformed cop was holding my briefcase
up.

Three

I turned, and with my hat pulled low and my hands stuffed in my pockets, headed away from the neighborhood as several sirens seemed to be converging on me from a distance.

Everything was suddenly going bad at once, and I wondered if we had spent enough time planning this operation.

When I had seen the ambulance attendants loading the body, I had figured the old man and his partner must have had a falling out over the money I was supposedly missing, and one of them had killed the other.

Why the cops had searched the roof, however, was beyond me. But they had, and they had come up with my briefcase. Once they got a look inside there'd be some bright boy downtown who'd put two and two together and make the connection between the papers and my escape from Bethesda.

From that point it would be like ten pins. Within a few hours my fingerprints from Dr. Wells' car would be sent up here and matched with the prints lifted from my room.

If they worked quickly, without too many snafus, they might put it all together within eighteen to twenty-four hours.

Saul Breitlow was the FBI's chief investigator here in New York, and once he got involved with the case it would go very quickly. I had seen his work, some of it at close hand, and he was damned good.

That meant I'd have to be out of the city by morning at the latest. Beyond that time the airports, bus and train depots, and car rental agencies would all be too risky for me to use.

That also meant I either struck gold with Yushenko tonight, or I would have to abandon him as a means of getting to Kobelev.

I had expected troubles along the way, but I had not expected anything like this so soon. If it had not been for the old man snooping around my room, everything would have been all right. And yet I found myself feeling sorry for him, if he was the one on the way to the morgue.

Three blocks away I boarded a bus, and fifteen minutes later I had gotten off on Kenmare Street in Little Italy, found a small Italian restaurant, and was seated in one of the back booths sipping a glass of cheap Chianti and waiting for my order of spaghetti to come.

I still couldn't figure out how they had found the briefcase on the roof. If the old man had been murdered the cops might have looked for a weapon. But why on the roof, and how come so quickly?

The question kept hammering at me, and the more I thought about it the less sense it made. Killers just didn't stop to hide weapons in ventilator shafts. So the police never bothered to look there, unless they had been tipped off.

My spaghetti finally came, and I ordered another glass of wine. Before the waiter would bring it to me, however, he asked to see my money. For an instant I almost snapped at him, until I realized that I was dressed like a bum with a couple of days' growth of whiskers on my face, and I had to smile.

I pulled out a ten dollar bill, and laid it on the table. "Enough?" I asked.

"Yes, sir," the man said crisply, and within seconds he had returned with my wine, and asked how I was enjoying my meal.

At one end of the restaurant was a long bar, above which, on a shelf, a television was playing. I had noticed the TV set on my way in but had paid it no further attention, more intent on trying to figure out how the briefcase had been found so quickly.

It was going to be difficult convincing Yushenko that I had more to offer in trade for political asylum without the additional files I had promised. But it was going to be even tougher convincing Kobelev . . . if I ever got that far . . . that I wasn't some stumblebum who couldn't do anything right.

I laid my fork down and as I picked up my wine glass to take a sip I happened to glance up. Several of the men at the bar were looking my way, and when they realized that I was watching them, they turned around.

I peered around the edge of the booth, at the tables and other booths in the restaurant, but the few people who had been here when I came in were gone now.

Something was wrong. Drastically wrong. Alarm bells jangled along my nerves.

I slid out from the booth and got to my feet as the bartender was reaching up to turn off the tele-

vision set. Two of the men climbed down from
their barstools and hurried out the door as I came
into the barroom.

"Leave it," I said to the bartender as he
stretched to reach the television's on-off switch. It
was evidently a news show of some kind. But that
was all wrong too. It was quarter of two in the afternoon. There were no news shows on at that
time. Only news bulletins.

I stepped farther into the bar as my photograph
flashed on the television screen. They knew! Christ,
they had traced me here already! And suddenly I
had a very strong hunch just how they had done it.

The bartender had stepped away from the television set and he started to reach around behind
him toward a drawer in the back bar below the bottles.

In a few long strides I was at the bar, the Luger
in my right hand. "Don't," I said softly, and the
bartender froze where he stood.

Three other men at the bar were all staring at
me, open-mouthed, none of them moving so much
as a muscle.

"Did you call the police?" I asked, keeping my
voice very soft.

The bartender just stared at me as if I were
speaking a foreign language. I raised the Luger a
little higher.

"If I hear the sound of a siren I will shoot you
all, and then leave."

"He called 'em, mister," one of the men at the
bar blurted drunkenly.

"How long ago?" I snapped.

"Just a minute ago . . . honest," the bartender
stammered. "Your picture came on the television.

Said you was a spy. I had to call 'em. You gotta understand."

Keeping my eye on the four of them I hurried sideways to the front door and opened it a crack. I could hear sirens, a lot of them, and not too far away.

"Stick your head out the door and I'll put a bullet between your eyes," I snapped at the bartender and his customers, and then I slipped outside as I stuffed the Luger in my pocket and headed down the street.

I got to the corner as two police cars, their lights flashing, sirens screaming, pulled up in front of the restaurant. Around the corner, out of sight of the police for a moment, I sprinted down the block, past a couple of startled women, and down the steps into the subway.

At the first level just below the street I leaped over the turnstiles, and raced down to the second level, someone shouting at me from above to stop.

There were half a dozen people on the platform waiting for the next train, and as I burst from the stairwell they looked my way.

"When's the next train due?" I shouted as I raced across toward the tracks.

No one said a thing until I jumped off the platform onto the track bed, and then a black woman stepped forward.

"You can't go down there," she said.

"Sure I can," I said looking up at her. I winked, and she smiled.

A uniformed policeman came from the stairwell, his gun drawn. "Stop!" he shouted.

"There's a train comin' . . . " the woman started to say, but I was racing down the tunnel into the

darkness, a faint rumbling coming from somewhere behind me.

As I hurried along the tracks I kept my left hand
out, brushing the tunnel wall. Often there were
alcoves or indentations in the walls which led to
maintenance doorways. The next boarding station
would probably be a couple of blocks farther down
the tracks, but judging by the sound of the rumbling behind me, which was rapidly increasing in
volume, I'd never make it that far.

I was beginning to sweat as I ran, and once I
stumbled and almost fell, catching myself at the
last moment.

A light stabbed the darkness from behind me a
few minutes later, and I looked over my shoulder
as the rumbling became even louder, filling the
confines of the tunnel with a huge, echoing roar,
and I put on an extra burst of speed.

The train would stop at the station behind me
for less than a minute, I figured. And then it
wouldn't take very long to catch up with me.

The tunnel curved to the left about fifty yards
ahead and I could just make out a dim light coming
from somewhere beyond it. I had already covered
at least a block, and it was possible . . . just possible, that the light was coming from another station.

My heart was pounding nearly out of my chest
as I reached the sweeping curve at the same moment the rumbling increased in volume again from
behind me and the train's headlight wavered and
danced in the darkness.

Another twenty-five yards and I was around the
curve, the station less than a hundred feet farther.

The noise of the approaching train was so loud

now that it blotted out all other sounds, making it nearly impossible for me to think. The air in front of my eyes seemed to waver and dance.

At the last moment I knew there was no way I could possibly make it up into the station itself, so I dove to the left where the tunnel widened slightly beneath the lip of the boarding platform, and then the train was on me with an incredible cacophony of sound and warmth and oil smells.

I flattened myself against the grimy cement wall as the train rumbled to a halt, the wheels inches away from my back.

If the engineer had spotted me running down the tracks he would be telling the police right now. I just hoped that the cop who had chased me down to the platform had not himself been caught in the tunnel.

I could hear the sounds of people getting on and off the train, and someone was shouting something less than four feet above me, but I couldn't quite make it out over the other noises.

After a seeming eternity the doors hissed closed, and the train began moving away, the sound once again building to an incredible level, shaking and vibrating everything.

Finally the last car had passed me, receding into the dark tunnel, and the noise began to fade.

Someone on the platform above flipped on a flashlight and shined it down the tunnel just as I was about to get up on my knees. Once again I flattened myself against the wall, and froze in that position.

"He didn't come up here, and he wasn't on the train," a man said.

"You're sure you saw him jump off the platform?" another man said.

"A hundred percent. He came this way. I saw that too."

"Jesus," the other one said after a hesitation. "He's probably spread all over the tracks back there."

"We're going to have to take a look," the first one said.

"Yeah. Let's get it over with."

There were the sounds of footsteps along the platform and then a uniformed cop jumped down onto the track bed less than five feet from where I lay. A moment later a second cop joined him, and together they headed down the tunnel, their flashlights bobbing and reflecting off the tracks. Within a minute they were both out of sight around the curve.

I lay there a few seconds longer, straining to hear if there was anyone else above. The station was quiet, and I slowly stretched up and peered over the edge.

The platform was deserted, and without further hesitation I climbed up and raced for the stairs, brushing off my filthy clothes as I ran.

At the second level I slowed to a walk as a woman and two children came down from the street, and then I was outside.

Sirens seemed to be coming from everywhere now, but for the moment there were no cops in sight on the street. It wouldn't take very long, however, for the two below in the tunnel to discover that my body wasn't there, and figure out that I had gotten away somehow.

Their walkie-talkies would not work below street level, which meant they'd have to come up either from this station or the one I had started from in order to sound the alarm.

It would give me a few precious minutes to get away from the center of activity. But I was going to have to get under cover very quickly. I had lost my hat, I was wet from being outside in the rain, and I was filthy with grease and dirt from the tunnel.

There were very few people on the streets and traffic was light as I headed down Grand to Mercer and then worked my way up into Soho, an area of narrow, filthy streets, little shops, restaurants, and apartment buildings.

Most people were at work at this time of the afternoon, but within a couple of hours the rush would be on.

Several times I saw police cars, but always at a distance and still converging on the subway station where I had last been seen.

Soon their search would spread outward, so as I walked I kept looking for a way out, some way for me to get under cover and then continue my unfinished business with Yushenko.

I found it finally on Spring Street just off Mercer. In the basement window of a five-story apartment building was a "For Rent" sign. A young man, probably in his late twenties, only slightly smaller than me, was coming up the steps carrying a trash can.

I crossed the street to him as he was setting the can on the curb, and he looked up suspiciously as I approached.

"You have an apartment for rent? I asked.

The man just looked at me, not saying anything at first. Finally he nodded. "That's what the sign says."

I reached in my pocket and took out a couple hundred dollars. "You'll never believe what happened to me on the way over here . . . " I started to say, but the man shook his head.

"Get out of here," he snapped, and he started to turn around.

I pulled the Luger out of my shoulder holster and pointed it at him. "Downstairs," I said.

The man looked at me and at the gun for a long second. "Shit," he said. "You were on television."

"Lets go," I said. "I don't want to hurt you."

"Shit," he said again, and he turned and shuffled down the stairs into the small but immaculate apartment below.

The living room was long and narrow, a doorway at the far end leading into the kitchen. I could see the door to another room beyond it.

"What's beyond the kitchen?" I asked.

"The bedroom."

"Anyone else here besides you?"

The man shook his head.

"You expecting anyone?"

He shook his head again.

"If someone comes to the door, there'll be trouble unless I'm expecting them."

"My wife will be home in a couple of hours. What do you want with us?"

"Nothing much," I said. "And in two hours I'll be long gone."

"What do you want?" he repeated.

"Back to the bedroom," I said. We crossed the living room, went through the kitchen, and entered a small bedroom where I had the man lay face down on the floor with his hands behind his back.

From the closet, which was stuffed with men's

clothes on one side and women's on the other, I grabbed half a dozen ties from a rack, stuffed the gun in my holster, and quickly tied the man's wrists and then ankles together. Next I tied a couple of ties together, looped one end around his neck and tied the other to his ankles. He'd be uncomfortable until his wife came home and untied him, but he would not be going anywhere.

I tied another tie around his eyes as a blindfold, and from a drawer in a bureau found a pair of clean socks which I stuffed in his mouth.

"I'll be out of here in a half hour," I told him. "And if you just lay there nothing will happen to you."

Working fast, I went back into the living room where I made sure the front door was locked and took the "For Rent" sign out of the window. In the bathroom I finally stripped off my soggy clothes, and took a hot shower and shave.

All that took less than fifteen minutes, and when I was finished I went back into the bedroom and dressed in a pair of corduroy slacks, a thick sweater, hiking shoes and a hooded rain jacket.

I'd have to get rid of the jacket at least, as soon as possible, because once his wife came home and released him he would call my description in to the police.

I left a couple of hundred dollars on the bed, which I figured would be more than enough to pay for the clothes I had taken and the trouble I had put him through. In the living room, I ripped the telephone cord out of the wall and let myself out.

Back on Spring Street I headed over to Broadway, where I hailed a cab and headed back uptown, police cars seemingly everywhere.

"Where you headed?" the cabby asked me as he pulled out into traffice.

"Forty-second and Third," I said sitting back. "What's going on with all the cops?"

The cabby shook his head. "Just heard that a couple of beat cops were chasin' someone down the subway tunnel and got caught by a special. It's a mess, from what my dispatcher said he heard. His brother-in-law is out of the Forty-eighth Precinct . . ."

The driver was rambling on with his story about how half his dispatcher's relatives were cops and the other half were crooks, but I wasn't really listening to him. Instead I was thinking about the two cops. I had watched them head down the tunnel.

I hadn't even really begun this mission and already people were starting to get killed. The more I thought about it, the blacker my anger became for Kobelev, and for Yushenko whose mechanations, I was fairly certain, had caused all this.

It was nearly three-thirty, but instead of the eighteen or twenty hours I had figured I would have, I reduced that estimate now to two or three hours.

When the man's wife returned home around five or five-thirty they'd immediately call the police. By six, or perhaps a little later, the police would realize I was no longer dressed as a bum. And every cop in the city would be on the lookout for me.

Yushenko left the U.N. building at six o'clock sharp. It would be cutting it close, to be out in the open then, but I had no other choice now. Getting out of the city was going to become very difficult and very soon.

The cabby left me off on Forty-second, and after

Four

It was six-thirty and Yushenko had not come out of the United Nations building. The crowd of secretaries, translators, and delegates to the various missions had rapidly dispersed because of the heavy rain. All the cabs were gone as well.

I stood beneath a city bus stop shelter half a block down from the main gate. The man might have simply skipped with the files I had handed over to his people this noon. Or he might have taken them down to the Soviet Embassy in Washington.

For some reason, however, I didn't think he had done anything like that. Not yet. He was probably at his apartment or still in his office, afraid to move until I had been picked up.

I was also reasonably certain that Yushenko had blown the whistle on me. Unless he was an exceedingly stupid man, I could not figure out why he had done it.

About twenty-five feet from where I stood was a pay telephone. I stepped out from beneath the shelter and went to the phone where I dialed Yushenko's home number. It rang five times before I hung up.

I turned and looked down the block toward the main gate, then shoved the dime in the slot and dialed another number which was answered on the second ring by a woman with a singsong oriental voice.

"Good evening, this is the United Nations, may I have your call?"

"Connect me with Oleg Yushenko," I said. "He's with the Soviet Trade Delegation."

"I am sorry, sir, but I believe Mr. Yushenko has left for the day. May I take a message?"

"Try his office, please," I insisted.

"Yes, sir," the woman said, and a second later the connection was made and Yushenko's phone was ringing.

It was answered almost immediately by Yushenko himself. "Yes."

"Greetings, Oleg Dmitrevich," I said softly.

"Who is this . . ." he started to say, but then swallowed his words.

"That's right," I said. "I'm waiting for you."

"Where are you?" he asked. He sounded worried.

"So you can tip off the police?"

"Don't be a fool, this is an open line," the man snapped.

"Why did you do it, comrade?" I said. "The Puppet Master won't be too happy with you."

He didn't say anything at first, but I could hear him breathing, and in the background it sounded like someone was arguing. "It was a mistake," he said, his voice guarded. "It happened before I got a chance to look at your . . . present."

I laughed. "They found the others. And that's going to make the Puppet Master very unhappy."

"You must be insane. This is an open line. We have to meet. Now tell me where you are," Yushenko said. There was a note of desperation in his voice.

He was ready. "Leave your office immediately. Call no one. Tell no one where you are going. Then walk up Forty-second Street. If you're clean I'll make contact."

"I'll have someone pick you up . . . " he was saying, but I hung up the phone and walked immediately down to Forty-third, and in less than ten minutes I was standing beneath the Vanderbilt Avenue viaduct on Forty-second across from Grand Central Station, waiting for him to pass.

The rain had begun to lessen but the wind had picked up and it was bitterly cold now. The few people on foot hurried with heads down into the wind. Across the street a couple of uniformed cops stood near the entrance to the train depot, talking with each other, their raincoats slick.

The four-door tan Chevrolet that had shown up at Washington Square came slowly down Forty-second Street, and as soon as it passed I stepped out from under the viaduct and started walking slowly in the same direction, stopping frequently to look in the windows of the various shops and stores.

Yushenko was taking no chances with his personal safety, and I wondered if the man was capable of doing anything without his henchmen being nearby.

Obviously they were in the Chevy, sweeping Forty-second, trying to pick me out before I made contact with their boss.

About a block before the Public Library, I saw

the reflection of the car in the window glass of a luggage store I stood in front of, and moments after it passed Yushenko walked by.

I turned and quickly fell in step beside him. he glanced over at me, his eyes instantly widening in recognition, and he started to look toward the Chevy now a half a block away.

"If you signal your friends I'll kill you right now," I said softly.

Yushenko started to say something, but then clamped his mouth shut and nodded.

"Why did you call the police after I contacted you?" I asked.

"I thought it was a set-up to compromise me," he said after a moment.

"And now?"

"I'm not so sure."

I laughed. "It still may be, comrade, as far as you know, but that's beside the point. Until the business with the police came up I thought to defect. But now, if everyone in the KGB is as goddamned inept as you seem to be, I'm not so sure."

Yushenko's eyes narrowed, but before he could say a thing I continued. "Have you been in contact with Kobelev yet?"

"I don't know anyone by that name."

"You don't know the Puppet Master? Nikolai Fedor Kobelev?" I said. "You're either a poor liar or a damned bigger fool than I thought you were."

"How do I know this isn't a trap?" he said. He was frightened. "How do I know you're not with the CIA?"

"I am, you idiot," I shouted, but then immediately lowered my voice. "Or I was until the bastards had me arrested for doing my job."

"And on that basis I'm to believe you're ready to defect?" Yushenko said.

I shook my head. "The hell with you," I snapped, and I turned off down Fifth Avenue past the Public Library, not bothering to look back to see what Yushenko was doing.

At the corner of Fortieth again, I started across the street when the tan Chevrolet pulled up beside me and the back door came open.

"Get in," Yushenko said from inside.

There were two other men besides Yushenko in the car, and I recognized the one on the passenger side of the front seat as the Russian I had handed the files to this afternoon at Washington Square.

I took a step backwards, hesitating for a moment, but then the traffic light changed and a cab behind the Chevy honked its horn. I stepped off the curb and jumped into the back seat, closing the door as we smoothly accelerated around the corner east down Fortieth toward the Queens Midtown Tunnel.

"Where are we going?" I asked.

Yushenko just glanced at me, the fear now out of his eyes, but he was sweating.

"*Anyone behind us yet?*" he asked the driver in Russian.

"*No,*" the man said, and Yushenko turned back to me.

"If anyone shows up behind us, Mr. Carter, you are a dead man. Immediately dead. Do I make myself clear?"

"There'll be no one back there unless you've bungled it," I said. "And if you have, Kobelev will hear about it."

Without warning Yushenko backhanded me

across the face. Instantly I reached for my Luger, but the man in the front seat leaned back and tapped my shoulder with the barrel of a .44 Magnum, a huge silencer screwed on the end of the muzzle. It looked like an artillery piece.

"I will ask the questions here, Mr. Carter," Yushenko said.

The blood had rushed to my face, and I made it obvious that I was fighting hard for control, forcing myself to sit back in the seat.

"Now carefully remove your weapon from its holster," Yushenko said. I started to reach inside my coat, but he held up a finger. "Carefully, or Stanislav Antonovich will make a very large hole in you."

I glanced at the man in the front seat, and then slowly pulled the Luger out of my holster and handed it to Yushenko, butt first.

He took the gun, looked at it for a moment, and then stuffed it in the pocket of his raincoat. "Anything else?" he asked.

For a second I hesitated, but then carefully slipped Hugo from his chamois sheath strapped to my left forearm beneath the sweater I was wearing, and held it out to him, handle first.

He shrank away from it, and after several tense seconds I handed the knife to the man in the front seat who took it almost reverently.

"You have killed with this?" he asked softly.

"Yes," I said. "And will again. For Kobelev."

Yushenko flinched.

"Now where are we going?" I snapped.

"Someplace where we can talk," Yushenko said.

"Good," I said, once again settling back in the

seat. "I've got plenty to talk about. Fifteen years worth as a matter of fact."

After the Midtown Tunnel we headed through Queens toward Kennedy International Airport, and for a while I was half convinced that Yushenko was actually going to try to get me out of New York that way. Now that the police had my description and were looking for me in earnest, it would have been suicide for all of us to attempt it.

But just before the airport the driver turned off the Van Wyck Expressway and headed east through Nassau, as darkness came and the rain finally turned to snow and sleet.

The driver was an expert, and despite the fact that the roads were becoming ice-covered and slippery, he did not slow down, keeping exactly to the speed limits through the towns and out on the stretches of open highway. Several times the Chevy began to fishtail, but he efficiently steered into the slide, instantly recovering control.

For a long time no one said a thing, but finally, a few miles before Southampton, Yushenko sat forward and spoke in Russian to the driver.

Will we be able to get back into the city tonight?"

"Yes, sir," the driver said. *"Although it may take longer than you wished."*

"Tonight's meeting is of no consequence," Yushenko said sitting back. *"Tomorrow morning I would be missed, however."*

He looked at me. "We have a house outside Montauk. I will have to leave you and Stanislav there tonight. But I will return tomorrow evening to begin your debriefing."

"You'll be at your office tomorrow?" I asked.

Yushenko looked at me for a long time before he nodded. "Yes."

"Good," I said. "Then you can get a message off to Kobelev for me."

He stiffened, but before he could reply I quickly continued.

"Tell him that I was the one involved in the *Akai Maru* business."

"What is that supposed to mean?"

I smiled. "You get the message off to Kobelev and he will understand."

"As I told you before, I do not know anyone by the name of Kobelev," Yushenko said.

"And as I told you before, comrade, you are either a terrible liar or a bigger fool than I thought you were."

He struck out at me again, but this time I was ready for him and caught his hand as it swung around and bent it backwards. "If you've had a chance to look at the files I passed over, you'll know they are genuine and important," I snapped.

Yushenko was squirming in his seat trying to pull out of my grip, and a second later the big Russian in the front seat had placed the barrel of the Magnum against my temple.

"Kill me and you'll have to answer to Kobelev," I said without releasing Yushenko's hand. "I'm genuine and I have a lot of information to pass. But much of it is for the Puppet Master's ears only."

"Release him or I will shoot you now," the big Russian said quietly.

This was it, I thought. The moment of truth. If I could get over this hump, I would be safe at least until a message was sent to Kobelev.

"In ten days Nikolai Kobelev will be promoted to chief administrator for the entire KGB," I blurted. "Think not only of what that means, but how I have come by that information."

Yushenko's eyes went wide, and he stopped struggling against my grip.

"Release him," the big Russian said, and he jammed the Magnum's barrel a little harder against my head.

Yushenko shook his head. "No," he squawked. "Do not shoot!"

The driver's attention had not diverted from the road, and I marveled at his concentration. For several long seconds the three of us sat frozen to our spots, until finally Stanislav eased the gun away from my head.

Carefully I released my grip on Yushenko's hand and then took a cigarette from my pocket, lit it, and inhaled deeply. "Never raise your hand to me again," I said calmly. "Or I will kill you."

Yushenko said nothing.

"Will you contact Kobelev with my message about the *Akai Maru,* or am I wasting my time with you?"

Yushenko nodded. "I will send the message," he said, his voice barely audible. "I will contact him. And if you are lying, your death will be a particularly unpleasant one."

"I will give you no trouble, comrade," I said looking into his eyes. "The reason I contacted you was because I want to defect. I have long admired Kobelev. I want to work for him." I turned to look at the man in the front seat. "I have many skills to offer."

The man smiled. "I believe you do. I hope you are not lying to us. Because if you are, believe me, we will find out and you will live to regret it."

Intelligence services operating in foreign countries the world over maintain what in the trade are called "safe houses." AXE, as well as the CIA, maintain their own safe houses in the world's capitals, from Paris to Tokyo, from Buenos Aires to Moscow. Although not always "houses" in the strictest sense of the word, they are places that have usually been purchased or rented through complicated strings of intermediaries, and are used for meetings where there are no chances for detection by the opposition.

Often, however, safe houses are places of electronic marvels, every room bugged so that idle comments as well as interrogations and meetings can be recorded.

The KGB is no different.

AXE knew, for instance, that the KGB maintains safe houses in San Francisco, Chicago, Washington, D. C., and New York. But this one at Montauk, came as a complete surprise to me. I had seen no mention of it on any of our circulars, nor had it been listed in the New York Foreign Operations manual I had studied when during the planning stages of this mission, Yushenko had been selected as my probable contact.

The house itself was a two-story colonial mansion that lay just outside of Montauk, on the northwest corner of Fort Pond, less than five hundred yards from Block Island Sound.

We pulled up the driveway, the snow coming

down hard and blowing almost horizontally in the stiff wind.

"I'm going back to the city now," Yushenko said to me. "Stanislav Antonovich has orders to kill you if you make any move to escape or attempt to communicate with anyone on the outside."

"I didn't come to New York to escape you," I said. "I came to escape the Company."

"All well and good if you are telling the truth, although I have my doubts. What Comrade Kobelev will say about you is another matter."

At least Yushenko would send my message.

The *Akai Maru* was a Japanese oil tanker out of Kuwait. Kobelev had maneuvered a Lebanese terrorist group into stealing a canister of highly radioactive strontium 90, which was dumped into the oil. I had stopped the operation, and covered up the entire episode so that no word was leaked as to what had really happened aboard. But once Kobelev got the message that I knew about the *Akai Maru,* he would have to see me.

"You will be comfortable, I assure you," Yushenko was saying. "I'll return tomorrow evening to begin your debriefing."

"When will I be taken to Moscow?" I asked.

"In due time, Mr. Carter, in due time," he said.

The big Russian in the front seat got out of the car and opened the back door on my side. Instantly, the car was filled with the cold, howling wind.

"A last word of caution," Yushenko said. He had to raise his voice over the wind. "Although Stanislav Antonovich is not very bright, he is a skilled and highly efficient killer. Behave yourself."

"Don't bungle the message, comrade," I said, and Yushenko's nostrils flared.

I climbed out of the car and slammed the door behind me. It pulled away, rounding the circular driveway, and was soon lost into the swirling snow.

For a while Stanislav Antonovich and I stood outside looking at each other. I was almost certain that he was thinking nearly the same thing as I was. If it came to a fight, just how good would the other be?

"He doesn't think very much of you," I said finally.

"It is of no consequence," the big Russian said.

Despite myself I found that I liked the man. He could have worked for AXE or the SDECE, or MI9 or the Mossad, or any intelligence service. The fact that he was with the KGB was nothing more than a geographical accident of birth.

"If I give you my word that I'll cause no trouble, that I won't try to escape, and that I won't try to contact anyone, can we relax?"

"You're a traitor to your own country," he shouted over the wind.

For an instant I had the insane desire to tell this man everything. "I hope you never have a change of heart and decide to defect. It'll ruin you."

"I don't trust you, Carter," he said. "You're lying. I can feel it, although no one will listen to me."

"Are we going to end up fighting, Stanislav Antonovich?" I asked.

"Probably," he said.

"That's too bad, because I will kill you even though I like you."

He threw back his head and laughed. "It will be something when it happens," he said.

We turned, went up the snow-covered walkway, mounted the steps to the porch, and went inside. The house was warm. A fire was burning in the fireplace across the entryway to the huge living room, and there was a smell of food cooking.

For a second the big Russian stood completely still just inside the doorway, but then he pulled out his gun.

"What is it?" I asked.

"A trap, perhaps," he said softly.

"Trap?" I said. "We know about most of your safe houses, but not this one," I said. "Besides, our people are terrible cooks."

"Oleg Dmitrevich, is that you?" a woman called from upstairs.

Stanislav took a step farther into the wide vestibule.

"Demi, don't play games with me," the woman called down. "It scares me."

"Yushenko's girlfriend?" I asked softly. "Could she have come out here without him knowing about it?"

The big Russian turned to me. "If it is a trap you are dead. If it is Oleg Dmitrevich's whore, she is dead."

"What about the girl?" I asked, knowing full well what the answer *had* to be.

"Demi?" the woman called, her voice coming now from the head of the stairs.

Stanislav moved quietly to the left as the woman started down the stairs, and he took up a position so that he could watch me as well as the stairs.

"Demi?" the woman called again. Then she came into view.

She was tall and willowly, with a model's figure, her hair long and very red. She saw me first.

"Oh," she cried. She was wearing a very short nighty with no panties, and she covered herself with her hands. "Oh," she cried again.

For a second I thought the Russian was going to shoot her, but then he holstered his huge gun, and stepped into view.

"What are you doing here?" he shouted.

"God dammit," she screeched, and she turned and raced back up the stairs.

Five

"Who is she?" I asked.

Stanislav Antonovich had been staring up the stairs and he turned slowly now to look at me. "Cynthia Patterson. Oleg Dmitrevich's latest whore. Perhaps more."

"If she was working with me, do you think I would have had her come out here? Especially now that I've made contact?"

"Your target is not the fool Yushenko."

"Who then?" I asked.

"Kobelev," he answered, his voice low, yet with a very hard edge to it.

I laughed. "And now you're going to tell me that I'm defecting so that I can get to meet Kobelev. Perhaps I'll assassinate him. That's why I killed the two cops in the subway." I glanced up the stairs. "What part does she play in my little plot, then?"

"I don't know," he said deliberately. "Perhaps in order to force Yushenko into getting you to Moscow you needed a lever."

Yushenko was dead wrong . . . this man was definitely not stupid. "In that case," I said turning back to him, "I would have to kill you."

"Yes," he said, and then he grinned. "But not

yet. Our little trial will not begin until after Oleg Dmitrevich returns tomorrow evening and finds his girlfriend here. By then we will have a reply from Kobelev as well."

"How about tonight?"

"Tonight?" he said, his grin widening. "Tonight we will be friends. Just the three of us." He laughed. "Go upstairs and tell her to come down and finish cooking our supper. It smells good and I have not yet had my evening meal."

"What about you?"

"Her car has to be somewhere near. I'll just fix it so that if she decides to take a midnight drive she will not be able to."

I took off my hat and raincoat and laid them over the banister.

"The look on his face tomorrow evening will be splendid to behold," the big Russian said, laughing.

"He's your boss," I said. "What does that make you?"

"Tonight we will be friends, Carter," he said, the harsh edge back in his voice. He reached in his coat pocket and withdrew my stiletto. For several seconds he fingered the blade and then felt the heft of it. "A very light weapon."

"Good for speed in fighting," I said.

He looked up and then gently tossed it to me. I caught it by the handle.

"I hope you decide to use your little deadly toy," he said. "Perhaps tonight after all. Perhaps tomorrow before Oleg Dmitrevich arrives. It will soothe my conscience to kill you."

"And if I am better than you are?"

He stepped closer. "Your news about Comrade

Kobelev's promotion, although not unexpected, was stunning. When what you have said spreads to the upper levels of our organization, an intense curiostiy about you will arise. An unhealthy curiosity."

"I want to work with you, Stanislav," I said. "I do not want to kill you."

"Yushenko has stars in his eyes about you. He is convinced you will lead him into Kobelev's favor. But I do not for a moment believe you."

Very slowly I raised my left arm and slipped Hugo into his sheath. "Is there any brandy in this place?"

The big Russian smiled. "A truly excellent brandy, and an even better vodka. I will fix us a drink as soon as I attend to the woman's car."

He turned, strode across the vestibule, and went outside—the wind-blown snow swirling for a moment through the open door—and then he was gone.

Nothing had gone right on this assignment yet, I thought as I stood at the foot of the stairs. An old man had been murdered, two cops had been killed, one of Yushenko's henchmen was convinced that this was a set-up, and the girl upstairs would die unless I could figure out a way of getting her out of here without blowing my own mission.

I looked up toward the second floor landing and then started up. How badly did I want Kobelev? How important was this mission? So important that I could sacrifice the life of a girl who wanted to live a little dangerously by playing games with a Russian national?

At the head of the stairs I turned right down the corridor toward an open door. Almost immediately I felt a cold draft, perhaps from a window left open.

"Cynthia," I called out.

There was no answer, but a moment later I could hear a window banging and the sound of wind howling.

She had jumped! Christ, she had jumped. If Stanislav Antonovich ran across her outside he'd kill her immediately, no questions asked.

I raced down the corridor and burst into the large, luxurious bedroom just as the girl was starting to climb out an open window. She was dressed now in blue jeans and a thick sweater. Her feet were still bare.

I dashed across the room to her and grabbed her by the legs, then pulled her back inside. She tumbled over the windowsill, banging her head against the floor, but then leaped up, shoving me backwards. In the next instant she was on top of me, her long fingernails raking my face.

I kicked my left leg up and out, hooking my foot around her shin, and flipped her aside. I quickly rolled over on top of her, grabbed her arms and pinned them against the floor over her head.

She was a beautiful girl, but her face was now contorted into a terrible grimace as she continued to struggle wildly with me.

At first I thought she was angry, but then it dawned on me that she was simply frightened out of her mind. She moaned and cried, straining with all of her might to get away.

"If you try to leave here Stanislav will kill you," I said.

Her eyes bulged nearly out of their sockets. "Oh

God," she cried. "Oh God. I've ruined everything. He'll kill me."

"No he won't," I snapped. "Not if you do as I say."

"He'll kill me," she cried again. "He'll kill us all. Demi says he's crazy. He gets his kicks from killing people."

She had stopped her struggles at last, and I let go of her arms, got to my feet and helped her up. "What are you doing here?" I asked.

Her eyes were filled with tears and she shook her head. "I wanted to surprise him," she sobbed. "But I've ruined it. He'll kill us all."

"You've got to get ahold of yourself," I said as gently as I could. Her presence here was just one more thing that had gone sour on this assignment. But what could I do with her?

I couldn't let Santislav kill her. Nor could I let her go. Any "betrayal" on my part at this stage of the game would ruin everything.

"Yushenko will be back here tomorrow night," I said. "You've got to hang on until then. Stanislav won't do anything until his boss gets here."

"My car," she said. "You've got to help me get away."

I shook my head. "He's out there now fixing it so it won't run. If you tried to leave now he'd kill you for sure."

The room was getting ice-cold and snow had already begun to pile up on the carpet. I stepped over to the window and closed it. I've always been a sucker for a pretty face, but I wondered now if her presence here wasn't just a little too coincidental. Perhaps she was a plant, and by getting me to help her would prove that I was a fake.

I started to turn back to her when she bolted for the door.

"No," I shouted. I raced after her, and by the time I reached the corridor she was already halfway down the stairs. "Don't go outside," I shouted, reaching the head of the stairs.

She stumbled at the foot of the stairs, picked herself up, leaped across the vestibule, and threw open the front door.

Stanislav was standing there, his hair windblown and snow-covered, a grin on his face.

The girl screamed, and then, as if in slow-motion, slumped to the floor.

I stopped halfway down the stairs, and Stanislav's gaze went from the girl huddled at his feet up to me.

"Kill her and you and I will have our little contest right now," I said. "I don't think you want that."

"Oh?" he said dreamily. "Why not?"

"There is an off chance, Stanislav Antonovich, that I might be for real. Think of it. If I am, killing me would put you in a rather tight spot."

I came all the way down the stairs, crossed the vestibule, bent down and picked the girl up.

"What's going to happen now, is that I'm going to take this girl upstairs and put her to bed. Then you and I are going to have a couple of drinks together, a little dinner, and then I'm going to get some sleep. It's been a long day."

Without waiting for his reaction, I turned and went back up the stairs, where I put her to bed in the large room, pulling the covers up under her chin.

Her eyes were fluttering as I sat down on the edge of the bed and brushed the hair out of her face. A few seconds later she came around, focused on my face, tried to sit up, but then slumped back.

"When you feel up to it, come downstairs and have some dinner," I said. "Nothing will happen to you, I promise."

"Who are you," she asked.

"Nick Carter."

"What are you doing here?"

"None of your business little girl. None of this is. We've just got to figure a way of getting you out of here."

"Is Stanislav going to stay the night?" she asked.

"Yes," I said, and she tried to struggle out from under the covers, but I held her back. "He won't hurt you," I said.

She struggled a moment longer, but then settled back again.

"How long have you known Yushenko?" I asked.

"He's a kind man," she said. "I met him three months ago. Things weren't going so good for me, and he helped me out, no questions asked."

"Do you love him?" I asked.

She smiled. "No. But I like him. We're friends."

I shook my head. "How did you know about this place?" I asked.

"I've been out here lots of times with Demi . . . with Oleg. He even gave me my own key."

How Yushenko had lasted as long as he had in this business was beyond me. But he was definitely a doomed man now. Yet no matter what he was or wasn't he had been kind to this silly young girl. What a terrible waste it all was.

I got to my feet, but the girl pushed the covers aside, reached up and grabbed my arm.

"Don't go," she said.

I gently disengaged her hand from my arm, and pulled the covers back. "I won't be far," I said. "Get some rest, then come downstairs."

"Not with him down there," she shivered.

"Then I'll bring you something to eat later. Just don't try to leave. He'll follow you and kill you."

"I won't. Not as long as you're here."

I went downstairs, crossed the vestibule, and looked into the living room. Stanislav was not there, but the fire was still burning in the natural stone fireplace, and a couple of drinks were laid out on a drop-leaf cabinet in a bookcase.

"Stanislav?" I shouted, but there was no answer. The only noises were the crackling fire and the wind outside moaning under the eaves.

He hadn't left, I was reasonably certain about that. He was somewhere in the house, probably watching me, or at least listening, to see what I would do.

Every room in the house was undoubtedly wired for sound so that he knew everything the girl and I had said to each other. He would be waiting now for me to make my move. To make a mistake.

I went all the way into the living room where I took the glass of brandy from the sideboard, sniffed it carefully, and just barely wet my lips with the liquor.

It tasted excellent. There was no bitterness, no unexpected sweetness. Although there are poisons that are supposedly colorless, odorless, and taste-less, they nevertheless alter the taste of whatever they're put in. I hadn't really thought that poison would be Stanislav's method, but anything was possible.

The living room was large and very tastefully decorated, and I had to wonder how Yushenko had justified its great expense.

From everything else I had seen of the man, I expected that he had lied to his superiors about this place. Very seldom do the Russians indulge themselves with luxury, at least on an official level, except for their military hardware.

I wandered aimlessly around the living room as I sipped my drink, turning on a couple of the table lamps, stirring the fire with a poker, and fingering some of the books in a large, floor-to-ceiling arrangement of shelves.

Within five minutes I had picked out at least two highly sensitive, omni-directional microphones, and in the fireplace a wide angle camera lens.

If Stanislav was in the house's electronic center, he was not only listening to me, he was watching my every move.

When I had finished the drink, I laid the glass back on the sideboard, then went through the dining room into the kitchen.

A bottle of champagne was cooling in an ice bucket on the counter, two glasses laid out next to it. In the refrigerator were two salads, and in the oven, which had been set on warm, were two perfectly broiled steaks.

Cynthia had evidently expected Yushenko to show up at any moment, had cooked a meal, had changed into the sexy nightgown, and was hoping to surprise him.

It had been a long day, I was tired and hungry, and I suddenly found that I didn't really give a damn where Stanislav was hiding, or if he was indeed watching and listening to me.

Nothing much was going to happen, I suspected, until Yushenko returned sometime tomorrow afternoon or evening. And if Stanislav wanted to spend the night in front of a closed circuit television screen, I wasn't about to offer any objections.

I rummaged around the kitchen and came up with a large serving tray, plates, silverware, and napkins. To this I added the salads from the refrigerator, and the steaks from the oven and the champagne and glasses from the counter, then went back through the living room and started up the stairs.

A week and a half from now Kobelev would be promoted to chief of the entire KGB and would then become an untouchable.

One thing his government had, that none of the free-world governments could boast of, was the fact that the Soviet Union's leaders were absolutely safe from assassination. Or as safe as anyone could be, even in a police state.

Killing Kobelev now was going to be very difficult to accomplish. Getting close enough to kill him after his promotion would be impossible . . . or nearly so.

A week and a half was not a very long time, which was why I had exposed to Yushenko my knowledge of Kobelev's impending promotion, and why I had mentioned the *Akai Maru* incident. The first had jogged Yushenko into action; the second, I hoped, would pique Kobelev's curiosity enough to have him order my immediate transportation to Moscow.

Perhaps, I thought as I climbed the stairs with the heavily ladened tray, Kobelev was not quite so sure of his promotion as we were. Perhaps he wanted one more accomplishment under his belt, one more coup against the West to cement his favor with the Presidium. Perhaps I would be that accomplishment.

At the head of the stairs I turned right and went down to where I had left the girl, and, balancing the tray in one hand, opened the door to her room.

The room was dark and very cold. In the dim light from the corridor I could see that the bed-covers had been thrown back and the window was once again open.

She had jumped! I couldn't believe it. I was sure that she understood what would happen if she tried to escape.

I stepped into the room, set the tray on the bed, and then raced to the window and stuck my head outside.

The wind was blowing very hard now, the snow thick, and the visibility near zero.

Directly below the window was the roof of the small porch at the kitchen door. For a split second I stared at the snow that had piled on the roof. It was smooth, blown into a gently sweeping drift against the side of the house. Smooth. She had not jumped.

I started to pull back inside when the barrel of a small automatic was pressed against my head just behind my ear.

"If you move I'll shoot you," Cynthia said in a shaky voice.

"I thought you had jumped," I said. It's one thing to have a professional holding a gun against your head. It's a totally different, and much more dangerous situation, when a frightened amateur's finger is on the trigger.

"Don't move," she shouted.

"Are you going to freeze me to death, Cynthia?" I asked, keeping the tone of my voice as light as possible. "Stanislav would just love it."

"I . . . don't know what to do," she cried.

"The steaks are getting cold," I said, tensing my muscles.

The barrel of the automatic slid a couple of inches to the left, and I jerked to the right, then swiveled around and grabbed her hand as the gun went off, the muzzle flash burning my neck.

She pulled away from me and jumped back, a horrified expression on her face. "God . . . oh God," she stuttered. "I almost . . . killed you."

The burn was superficial, but it hurt and it made me mad. This girl was trying her damnedest to get herself killed, despite my best efforts.

I took a step toward her, and she shrank back.

"I'm sorry," she wailed.

I shook my head. "If you want to die, Cynthia, you don't have to force Stanislav into doing it. You can do it yourself."

I released the catch into the safety position, and then tossed the little automatic to her. She caught it with fumbling hands as I closed the window and locked it.

When I turned back to her, she was holding the gun in both hands, staring down at it. Yushenko was a fool, and he had apparently come up with a well-suited match.

I brushed past her and strode out into the corridor. At the head of the stairs I looked back. She was standing in the doorway looking at me, tears in her eyes. "I'm sorry," she said in a small voice.

"Go back into your room and lock the door," I said gently. "I don't think Stanislav will bother you tonight, but don't let anyone in. I'll bring you something more to eat in the morning."

"Nick . . . " she said.

"Go on. If he tries to get in, shoot him. I'll explain everything to Yushenko tomorrow afternoon when he gets here."

I turned and went down the stairs. Before I hit the bottom I heard the door close and the lock snap. She would be safe for tonight, but tomorrow was another matter.

Back in the living room I put a couple of logs on the fire, put a few records on the expensive stereo set up in one corner, and then poured myself a couple of fingers of brandy which I drank down in one swallow.

It was very possible, I thought morosely, that Yushenko's girl friend could ruin everything. There was no way I was going to stand by and do nothing if and when Stanislav tried to kill her.

I poured myself another drink and turned as Stanislav came into the room. He was grinning.

I raised my glass to him and took a sip. "I thought maybe you had gone back to town," I said.

He laughed. "Why didn't you kill her?"

"I prefer my victims to be much bigger, and even more stupid," I said.

The smile left his face. "The windows and outside doors all are alarmed. If the bells should ring tonight, I will kill you first, and then the girl."

"I hope you sleep with one eye open, Stanislav Antonovich."

"I do," he said. "And now I am going to bed. Pleasant dreams." He turned, went back into the vestibule, and I could hear him climbing the stairs. A few moments later I could hear a door opening and closing, and then the house fell silent once again, except for the softly playing music, the crackling fire, and the wind outside.

I stood at the sideboard for a long time afterwards, sipping my drink, and wondering about Stanislav, Yushenko, and, most importantly, Kobelev. But finally I took the bottle over by the fire, kicked off my shoes and settled back in the overstuffed couch. I lit a cigarette and listened to the music and the wind that seemed to be playing a lonely duet.

Six

I was dreaming, and I knew it, but I could not help myself. I had just gotten out of a car and I was walking toward a house. It was in Washington suburbs, and I knew the place belonged to my boss Bob McKibbens.

The front door opened as I mounted the single step to the brick porch, and Elizabeth—Bob's wife —was grinning at me as she stepped aside to let me in.

As I came closer I could see the inside of the house. There were a number of people there, and although I was sure that I had never seen any of them before in my life, I was strangely aware that I knew them all. Knew them personally.

I raised my arm and looked at my watch. It was a few minutes past two A.M. For several seconds I stared at the luminous dial, not really knowing if this was a part of my dream or not. But then, slowly, I realized that I was awake, and I turned to look over at the fire which had died down to glowing embers.

I had turned out the lights and then lay down on the couch around midnight, I remembered, and had fallen asleep almost immediately.

A few wisps of the dream lingered on the edges of my conscious mind, but when I tried to focus on them, tried to recall what it was I had seen, they faded to nothing, leaving me with a vague feeling of unease.

I sat up finally. The stereo had shut itself off after the last record, and the house was quiet except for the wind that still howled outside. I shivered, got up and put a couple of logs on the fire, then padded into the kitchen and got a drink of water.

When I came back into the living room the logs had already begun to catch, the flames providing a gently wavering illumination to the room.

I went across to one of the windows and looked outside, but little was visible except for the blowing snow. For a long time I stood there thinking. The opening moves had been made, and if Yushenko had not been lying to me, a message had already been sent to Kobelev. Soon, I expected, and very soon, the next steps of this little dance would begin.

Once again my earlier doubts about my chances came bubbling to the surface, and I had to shake my head. Kobelev was good, probably the best in the business anywhere, and he had the instant support of the entire KGB at his beck and call.

On the other hand, I was nearly on my own. There were damned few people who knew what my real mission was all about. We had had to keep it that way in order to minimize the danger of leaks.

It was me alone against Kobelev and the

KGB. There would be no second chances.

Cynthia was standing in the doorway from the vestibule when I turned around. She was wearing a man's bathrobe, her feet bare and her hair disheveled.

"What are you doing down here?" I asked softly, not moving from where I stood.

She glanced over her shoulder at the stairs, then came all the way into the room. "I couldn't sleep," she said. I could see that she had been crying.

"Go on back to your room and lock the door. You'll be safer there."

"Is Demi . . . Oleg Dmitrevich a friend of yours?" she asked.

"I just met him."

"You're an American."

"That's right," I said. I moved away from the window, and picked up my glass and the brandy bottle by the couch and poured myself a drink.

"Can I have one of those?" the girl asked, taking a few hesitant steps closer to me.

What the hell was I going to do with her? Within fourteen hours or so, Yushenko would be back, and then all hell would break loose. A lot of what would happen would depend upon how deeply he felt for her, and how much control he really had over Stanislav. No matter what, though there *would* be trouble.

"Get yourself a glass," I said, motioning toward the sideboard.

She stared at me for several seconds, her lower lip quivering. "I'm sorry for what happened upstairs," she said in a very small voice. "Is your neck all right?"

"Fine," I said.

She took a step backwards, then turned and went over to the sideboard where she found a glass. She was shivering when she came back to where I was standing in front of the couch, and her hand shook as she held the glass out.

I poured two fingers of brandy into the snifter, then set the bottle down. She was now shivering so badly that she had to hold the glass in both hands to bring it to her lips and take a drink.

"Come and sit by the fire and finish your drink," I said. I reached out for her arm, but she flinched, spilling some of the liquor on the front of her robe.

"I'm not going to hurt you," I said. I took her arm and this time she did not resist as I gently guided her around to the fire and sat her down at the end of the couch.

"I'm frightened," she said looking up at me. Her eyes were large.

"What the hell are you doing here, Cynthia? Why did you pick Yushenko?"

She turned toward the fire and stared at the flames for a while. "I don't know," she said wistfully. "It just happened."

I sat down next to her. "Like in the movies?"

She turned back to me, her eyes glistening. "Don't make fun of me."

"I'm sorry," I said.

The tears began to slip down her cheeks as I took her drink and set it on the floor. She came into my arms, then, and sobbed.

I sat back, and stroked her hair as she cried herself out. There was one solution of course, but it would be very dangerous. I could kill

Stanislav tonight, help the girl get her car started and let her go. When Yushenko returned I could tell him that Stanislav had forced the fight.

Yushenko might not believe my story, and it would not work unless I could get at the video and sound recording equipment and erase the tapes.

All of that would put me in a very precarious position, made doubly dangerous by the fact that Cynthia would know I was here, and might go to the police with that information once she read in the newspaper how I supposedly was a murderer, and was responsible for the deaths of two New York policemen.

She pulled away from my shoulder, finally, and I brushed her hair away from her eyes and then dried her tears with my handkerchief.

The front of her bathrobe had parted, exposing her breasts. They were small and lovely, but I could not bring myself to take advantage of her. She was too vulnerable at the moment. I pulled the robe shut, then got up and helped her to her feet.

"I'm taking you back up to your room," I said.

"I don't want . . ."

"Do as I say, Cynthia," I said. "I want you to lock yourself in and no matter what happens tonight, keep your door closed."

"I want to stay here with you."

"No," I said. I led her around the couch, then across the room into the vestibule.

At the foot of the stairs she looked up, and then tried to pull away from me. "He's up there," she said. "I don't want to go upstairs."

"It'll be all right," I said. "I promise you."

"Please," she cried. "Please, I don't want to go up there." She was shaking again, and her eyes were filling with tears, her complexion pale. She was frightened out of her mind.

"All right," I said. "All right. You can stay down here."

"Where are you going to be?"

I glanced up toward the second floor landing. "Close," I said. If Stanislav had been monitoring our conversation he would be expecting me.

"Stay with me," the girl said.

I turned back to her. Was she worth the risk? Or was I kidding myself into believing I had a choice.

I have never turned my back on an assignment, no matter how difficult it became. But now, tonight, looking into the girl's eyes, I wondered what it was all about. I wondered what AXE's real purpose was. Perhaps we were nothing more than safety valves for the ineptitude of politicians.

Kill or be killed. It was as simple as that until an innocent bystander got in the way. Then it became much more complicated.

"I'm getting you out of here tonight," I said, finally making my decision. I took her by the arm and led her back into the living room, where once again I sat her down on the couch.

I knelt down in front of her. "I've got to ask you a couple of questions," I said.

She nodded uncertainly.

"Did Yushenko ever talk to you about tape recorders here in the house?"

She shook her head.

"He never said anything to you about microphones, or cameras?"

Again she shook her head. "I don't know what you're talking about."

"When you came here with him, did he ever disappear for a moment or two?"

"I don't . . . " she started to say, but then stopped in mid-sentence. "Once," she said, "when we were upstairs, and were going to make . . . when we were going to bed together, he got up and went down the hall to his room."

"His room?"

She nodded. "I saw him coming out of the room, and then he locked it. We laughed about it. He told me it was his private study. He called it his little blue room. Said he wanted to be alone every now and then. That's where he went then."

"You never saw the inside of the room?"

"No," she said.

"Where is it, exactly?"

"Across the hall from my room, two doors down. It's next to the bathroom."

It was probably the electronic center. Yushenko would have shut off the machines whenever he had her here.

"Listen to me, Cynthia," I said. She blinked. "I want you to stay right here. No matter what happens, no matter what you hear, stay right here until I return. Do you understand?"

She nodded uncertainly. "Where are you going?"

"Upstairs to get your clothes. And when I get back we're going to fix your car and you're going to drive back to the city."

"Tonight? In the dark?"

"As soon as it gets light," I said. I stood up. "Will you do as I say, and remain here?"

She nodded. "But what about Stanislav?"

"Don't worry about him."

She jumped up. "You're going to kill him, aren't you?"

"Listen little girl, I don't know if you understand what you've gotten yourself in the middle of, but I want you to sit down, keep your mouth shut, and watch the fire."

"Don't go . . . " she said, but I shoved her down on the couch.

"Don't move," I said. Then I went back out into the vestibule and moved silently up the stairs as I pulled Hugo from his sheath.

The landing was in semi-darkness, and as I reached the top of the stairway I crouched low, ready to spring right or left if I caught any sign that Stanislav was waiting for me.

But there was nothing. The corridor was empty, and for a moment I stood there hoping that the girl would remain where she was and not make any noise. When it came to a confrontation between Stanislav and me, the choice of time and place would be mine I hoped.

I hurried past the girl's room to the door she had said was Yushenko's private domain, and put my ear to it. I could just make out a faint whirring sound from within. Machinery of some kind, but if Stanislav were inside, or if the door was alarmed, the confrontation would come immediately.

A standard lever lock was set in a brass plate beneath the doorknob, and within a couple of seconds, using the tip of the stiletto, I had sprung the release mechanism and the bolt withdrew.

The house remained quiet. No alarms yet. Slowly I turned the knob, and then eased the door open, expecting at any moment for lights to flash and bells to clang. Though there were still no alarms sounded I knew for sure now that this was the monitoring center of the house. From within the room came the unmistakable odor of electronic equipment, and the whirring sound came from a reel-to-reel tape recorder and three video recorders.

I slipped inside the room, closing and locking the door behind me, and then flipped on the light switch.

The equipment was set up on a table in the tiny room that had probably once been used as a linen closet. Above the table was a switching panel, into which the various microphones and cameras were connected.

I sheathed the stiletto and crossed to the table where I studied the equipment for half a minute. Then I shut everything off, hit the rewind button on one of the tape recorders for a few seconds, and then the replay.

My voice came from the speaker. ". . . if you understand what you've gotten yourself in the middle of, but I want you to sit down, keep your mouth shut, and watch the fire."

"Don't go," the girl said, and then there was a rustling sound.

I shut the tape recorder off. It was all here. Everything that had been said and done from the moment Stanislav and I had arrived, and proba- bly even when the girl had shown up earlier had been recorded. Very likely the equipment was engineered to turn on the moment anyone entered the house.

But Cynthia had said Yushenko turned the equipment off whenever he and the girl were here and were going to make love.

I looked up and studied the control panel above the table for a few moments. It was a simple set-up, with inputs from the various rooms feeding into the panel, and from there down to the tape recording units. A cut-off switch for each room was located above the appropriate jack.

Quickly I flipped off the inputs for every room in the house, and then set the sound recorder and all three video recorders on rewind.

Yushenko was nothing but a fool. I was sure that Kobelev was aware of that, just as I was reasonably certain that Yushenko's superiors were aware of the fact that the man had one or more mistresses over here.

I was gambling that they would accept the possibility that Yushenko himself had shut off the inputs to the tape recorders some time ago, and had simply forgotten to turn them back on, so that when Stanislav and I had shown up, the machines had begun recording, but recording nothing.

It was weak, but I had no other choice right now. I could not destroy the equipment, or even sabotage it, because I would be the prime suspect.

It took nearly five minutes for the tape in all four machines to fully rewind, and I flipped each of them onto the RECORD mode. Once all the tape had run out, everything that had been recorded would be erased.

As I turned toward the door, bells started clanging through the house, and my first thought was that the crazy girl had opened the front door and was trying to get away.

I flipped off the light switch and eased the door open a crack in time to see Stanislav Antonovich, gun in hand, racing to the stairs and then heading down.

As soon as he was out of sight, I slipped out into the corridor and headed for the stairs, but stopped in mid-stride as Yushenko's voice came from below.

"We're getting out of here tonight," he shouted.

The girl was downstairs, and Yushenko was back! I raced back to the door, and again using the tip of the stiletto as a lock pick, relocked the door. Someone started up the stairs as I was finishing, and I raced down the corridor, and slipped quickly into the bathroom.

I splashed some water on my face, and then went back out into the hall, the bells still clanging.

Stanislav was just opening the door to the girl's room and when he saw me out of the corner of his eye, he spun around and dropped into a crouch, bringing the Magnum up on me.

I stopped in my tracks. "What's all the commotion?" I asked.

For several long seconds he stared at me, and then his eyes flickered to the electronic center door, as he slowly stood up.

"Where's the girl," he shouted over the noise of the alarms.

"Downstairs," I said. "By the fire. Now what the hell is going on?"

He came slowly down the corridor, the gun still trained on me, and at the electronic center door he tried the knob.

"She's not in there," I said impatiently. "She's downstairs. Now what the hell is going on, and shut off the damn bells, they're driving me crazy."

Almost before the words had left my mouth, the alarm bells ceased, and a moment later Yushenko called from downstairs.

"Stanislav Antonovich?"

"Up here," Stanislav called back.

We could hear Yushenko tramping up the stairs, muttering as he came. Evidently Cynthia had stayed put, and he had not seen her yet.

"Let the girl go," I said softly, but urgently.

The big Russian grinned. "Was she a good lay?"

"You bastard," I started to say, when Yushenko came to the head of the stairs.

"We must get out of here immediately," he shouted as he spotted us. Then he stopped in mid-stride as he realized that Stanislav was holding a gun on me. "What the hell is going on?"

"Why do we have to get out of here tonight?" I asked before Stanislav had a chance to speak.

Yushenko looked from me to Stanislav and back. "There's a Canadian-disguised trawler waiting twenty miles offshore. We've got to rendezvous before morning."

"There is a guest waiting for you downstairs, Oleg Dmitrevich," Stanislav snapped in Russian.

For a moment Yushenko was confused.

"What?" he asked in English.

"Your whore, Oleg Dmitrevich," the big Russian said. *"She is waiting for you."*

"Cynthia?" Yushenko stuttered.

"She doesn't know a thing Yushenko . . . " I shouted, but the man suddenly seemed to go crazy, and he turned on his heel as he pulled a pistol from beneath his coat, and headed back downstairs.

"Stop him!" I snapped at Stanislav in Russian.

He grinned again and lowered the Magnum. "Be my guest," he said.

For an instant I hung there, torn between the prospects of ruining this assignment and allowing Yushenko to kill the girl downstairs. But again, there was no real choice for me.

I leaped forward past Stanislav, and as I raced down the stairs three at a time I slipped my stiletto back out of its sheath.

"Yushenko!" I shouted. "Yushenko!"

The girl screamed as I hit the vestibule and leaped toward the door to the living room.

"You miserable bitch!" Yushenko screamed.

I burst into the living room at the same moment Yushenko was raising the gun directly at the girl, who was cowering behind the couch.

I flipped the stiletto around so that I was holding it by the blade, and in one smooth motion threw it with every ounce of my strength.

The knife buried itself in Yushenko's back at the same moment his pistol went off.

As he stumbled forward and fell over the back of the couch, the girl's head snapped back, a bright red spot appearing on her forehead, and much of the back of her head exploded outwards, blood, bone, and white matter splattering into the fire with a hissing noise and a sickening stench.

I took a couple of steps farther into the room, as Stanislav came to the doorway.

"Well done," he said.

I turned toward him. He had holstered his gun, and it took everything within me at that moment not to leap forward and kill him. Yushenko was dead, but there was a Soviet trawler apparently disguised as a Canadian fishing vessel offshore somewhere, that we were to rendezvous with.

A message must have already been sent to Kobelev, and a reply received. Kobelev. A vision of the man swam up into my mind's eye, and stayed my hand. At least for the moment.

Seven

The front door opened and closed. "In here, Mikhail," Stanislav said without taking his eyes off me.

"I thought I heard a gunshot," Yushenko's driver said, coming in from the vestibule. He stopped when he saw me standing there, and then his eyes strayed to Yushenko, Hugo protruding from his back, and the girl's body on the other side of the couch.

Almost instantly a gun was in his hand, pointed at me. "What is happening here?" he snapped.

The man's eyes widened slightly, but the gun never wavered.

"It was Oleg's whore," Stanislav said, glancing at the other man. "She was here when we showed up."

"How did she get in?"

"She had her own key," I answered. I turned very slowly, went over to where Yushenko lay sprawled next to the couch, and bent down beside him. There was no pulse at his neck. I looked over at Cynthia's body and shook my head. There was no doubt that she was dead. No doubt at all.

I started to pull my stiletto out of Yushenko's back.

"Do not touch your little toy," Stanislav said.

I turned and looked up at him. "You're no longer interested in our little contest then?"

"You want to see Comrade Kobelev. You will get your wish. I will see to it." He grinned.

I stood up. "What about their bodies? We can't leave them here."

"They're coming with us," Stanislav said. He turned to Yushenko's driver. "We'll take the boat out to the rendezvous and dump the bodies at sea. After we're gone, clean up here, close down the house, and get back to the city. The First Secretary will know what to do."

The other man looked at me for a long moment, but then holstered his weapon. "After you clear the Montauk Point Light, continue out for twenty miles on a heading of due east. Three longs and one short, repeated."

"What about the boat?" I asked. "Are you just going to leave it out there?"

"I'm not going with you," Stanislav said. "I must return and get rid of the girl's car. Not to worry, however, you will be well taken care of aboard ship."

Again I had the almost overwhelming urge to take both of these men out. But it would not have accomplished a thing. Certainly it would not help Cynthia, and it would ruin any chance I had of getting to Kobelev.

"Then let's get started," I said with disgust. "I'm tired of screwing around with amateurs."

Stanislav's jaw tightened. "Remain here," he said, and he turned on his heel and left the room.

I could hear him going upstairs as Yushenko's driver and I stood looking at each other, and then there was silence from above.

"Why did Comrade Yushenko kill her?" the man asked me.

I shrugged. "Because he was afraid of what would happen when Kobelev found out he had been bringing his girl friends out here."

The man shook his head. "He wasn't very smart, but he dressed well, and always had good-looking women."

"How will you explain his sudden disappearance to the authorities?"

"It's not my concern. The First Secretary will take care of it."

"What did he do with the files I passed over?"

The man's eyes narrowed. "You ask too many questions."

"I have a stake in this, comrade," I said. "I risked my life trying to make contact with you people. And then this idiot tipped off the New York City police. Now what the hell did he do with the files I passed over?"

"They were digested, microfilmed, and then the originals were destroyed," he said. "Standard procedure."

"For transmission?"

"That's enough," he said. Stanislav was coming down the stairs, and Yushenko's driver evidently figured he had said too much already. But he added at the last moment, "Be careful with Stanislav Antonovich."

"Thanks," I said, and then Stanislav came into the room.

He was wearing a military style parka, and carrying another one which he threw to me. "Put that on," he said. "You can carry the girl, I will take Oleg."

I pulled on the parka and zippered it up, then went around the couch for my shoes which I put on as Stanislav and the other man spoke to each other in very hushed voices. I couldn't quite make out what they were saying, except that it had something to do with communications.

"Is it very far?" I asked.

"A couple of hundred yards," Stanislav said. He came the rest of the way into the room, ripped the stiletto from Yushenko's back, wiped it off on the dead man's coat, and then pocketed it. "Let's go," he said.

I looked down at the girl. "Just a moment," I said. I stepped around the couch, went out into the vestibule and grabbed my raincoat from where I had laid it over the banister. Back in the living room I wrapped the girl's body in the coat, covering her head, and then picked her up. She was very light, her entire body liquid, almost as if she had no bones.

A bleak anger rose up inside of me as I thought about a young Israeli woman, probably the same age as this girl, who had also been killed because of Kobelev. It had happened during the incident on the *Akai Maru*.

I could understand any government wanting to field an intelligence network among its enemies. But Kobelev's mechanizations went beyond that. Destruction for destruction's sake seemed to be all he was really interested in.

Stanislav had picked up Yushenko's body and

threw it over his shoulder as if it were a rag doll, and together we went through the dining room into the kitchen and out the back door.

The other man closed and locked the door behind us, and within ten or twenty yards we had completely lost sight of the house in the blinding, wind-driven snow that had not abated in the slightest during the night.

Stanislav seemed to know where he was going in the dark. He never slowed down, nor did his step falter as we trudged through snow drifts sometimes as high as our knees.

After a while I began to hear another sound over the shrieking of the wind, though I couldn't immediately identify what I was hearing. Soon it dawned on me that I was listening to the ocean and the breakers rolling up on a nearby shore.

After ten minutes of walking a light finally appeared in the darkness ahead, and within a couple of minutes we had come to a set of wooden stairs that led down to a dock, a single, high-wattage lightbulb illuminating the first ten feet.

"Be careful," Stanislav shouted over the wind and surf. "It is slippery. I don't want to lose you here."

"Don't you slip either," I shouted.

He eyed me for a moment. "You first," he said.

I had to throw the girl's body over my shoulder so that I would have one hand free to hang on to the wide wooden railing as I descended down to the dock twenty-five feet below.

At the bottom the wooden planks of the dock were slick with ice. Spray from the incoming breakers soaked my feet and legs within a few seconds, and the wind here seemed much stronger than it had on top, making it very difficult for me to keep my footing.

About seventy-five feet out along the dock we came to a forty-foot fishing boat with an enclosed pilothouse and, I assumed, crews quarters below.

Stanislav literally threw Yushenko's body down onto the heaving deck of the ship, and it hit with a sickening thump.

Carefully I sat down on the edge of the dock, and timed the rise and fall of the boat's deck a few feet below me. As it reached the top of a swell I jumped down, slipped on a patch of ice and rolled to the right, Cynthia's body breaking loose from my grasp and flopping on top of Yushenko.

The coat I had wrapped her in came loose as did the bathrobe and she lay on her back, nude, the wind whipping at the clothing.

I scrambled over to her with the intention of rewrapping her body when Stanislav jumped down to the deck, grabbed my shoulder and spun me around.

"The whore is dead. Leave her lay," he shouted.

Finally, at long last, I had had it. For the moment, Stanislav embodied everything I hated, everything I had dedicated my entire life to fighting.

I was still crouched low, and using my legs as powerful springs, I drove upwards, smashing my shoulder into his chest like a battering ram. He slammed backwards against the pilot house, dazed for just an instant.

Before I could regain my balance, however, he swung a massive fist that caught me on the side of the head, sending me sprawling.

The thick padding of the parka hood had cushioned most of the blow and I was back on my feet immediately as Stanislav fumbled beneath his coat and started pulling out the .44 Magnum.

In two steps I was on him, kicking out with my right foot, catching him in the shin just below his left knee. As he started to go down, I grabbed the fur of his parka hood with both hands and propelled his head downward as I brought my knee up with every bit of strength I possessed.

The gun clattered to the heaving deck and skidded away from us as Stanislav bellowed, drove up under my guard, and grabbed me in a bear hug.

He straightened up, lifting me off my feet, and began to squeeze the breath out of my body. My arms were free and I managed to reach down and get both hands under his chin. I shoved upwards, bending his head way back, and quickly reached up with one hand to gouge my fingers into his eyes.

Again he bellowed in pain and rage. He tossed me halfway across the deck where I stumbled and fell backwards over Yushenko's and Cynthia's bodies.

Stanislav, my stiletto in his hand, was shaking his head, blood pouring from his nose as I got to my feet.

"So," he said thickly. "You made one fatal error after all."

I circled warily around the bodies, keeping low so that I could spring out of the way if he suddenly lunged at me.

"What was that?" I shouted over the wind. "Not killing you earlier tonight when I had the chance?"

Stanislav laughed. "That's not it at all. You made the assumption that I worked for Yushenko. He made the same error."

"Who do you work for then?" I asked. "The CIA?"

Stanislav began moving in toward me, and I continued circling to the left, toward the opposite side of the pilot house.

"The man you call the Puppet Master," the big Russian said, and for a second that stopped me.

Stanislav worked for Kobelev? What the hell was he doing attached to the United Nations? It didn't make any sense, unless Kobelev was planning some kind of a mission in New York. Either that or Stanislav was lying. But for what reason?

"You're lying," I shouted. "Either that or you're more stupid than I thought you were."

He lunged at that moment, and I leaped around the corner of the pilot house. Out of sight for just a split second, I spun around on my heel, planted my left foot as firmly as I could, and drove my right foot out and up with everything I had.

Stanislav came around the corner full tilt, as I had known he would, his legs spread as he ran, and the toe of the heavy hiking boot I was wearing caught him full in the crotch.

He screamed, dropped the stiletto, staggered backwards, and then doubled over.

I dropped down in front of him and grabbed the stiletto off the deck. But I had underestimated his strength and determination. Despite the intense pain he had to be in, he still managed to reach out and grab me by the head.

He started to twist my head around as I drove

the stiletto upwards, burying it to the hilt in his neck.

Blood spurted everywhere as he let go of me and jumped back, the blade ripping out of his neck as he did so.

He gurgled something, then turned and stumbled back a few paces and finally collapsed.

For several seconds I remained where I was, the stiletto in my hand, my parka sleeve soaked to the elbow in the man's blood. But then I slowly got to my feet and went to where he lay.

"Damn," I swore to myself.

I looked aft, beyond the boat out toward the sea, but nothing was visible except for the blackness and the swirling snow.

I would have to make the rendezvous myself, but before that I had to somehow get a message off to Hawk. If Stanislav was really working for Kobelev, then some mission had been planned for New York. Hawk would have to be informed, preparations made.

As I started to turn, something hard and very hot grazed my left leg just below the hip, sending me spinning and nearly pitching me over the rail into the sea.

Another shot whined off a metal fitting as I fell to the deck and rolled to the right, then lay still.

Mikhail, the other Russian, was on the dock less than twenty feet away. He got up from where he was crouched on one knee and headed closer.

I waited until the boat dropped to the bottom of the next swell, and then scrambled across the deck to where Stanislav's .44 Magnum lay.

Mikhail dropped to one knee again, brought his

gun up, and fired a shot that went wide. At that moment I had the Magnum up, waited for the boat to come up on the next swell, and squeezed off a shot.

The Russian seemed to leap off his feet, his hands going straight up over his head, and he fell backwards.

The old man in the apartment back in New York City. The two cops in the subway. Cynthia. Yushenko. Stanislav. And now Mikhail. Seven people dead already.

As I got painfully to my feet, I had the sinking feeling that there was going to be a lot more deaths before this was over. If it was ever over.

I picked my stiletto up from where I had dropped it, and shoved it back in its chamois sheath, then pocketed Stanislav's gun.

The wound on my leg hurt like hell, but there was very little blood. The bullet had only creased the skin. I'd be sore in the morning if I was still alive by then, but I could still walk.

After I had rewrapped Cynthia's body in the raincoat, I took it below and laid it on one of the bunks in the very spartan cabin. Then I brought Yushenko's and Stanislav's bodies below and laid them on bunks as well.

Back up top, I climbed painfully to the dock and dragged Mikhail's body to the boat and put it below decks as well.

I didn't know how long the trawler captain would remain standing by out there, but I expected he would wait at least until dawn. Kobelev had ordered me picked up. I didn't think a ship captain would dare argue.

First, however, I wanted to go back up to the house and telephone Hawk. He had to be informed that Kobelev had at least one of his people stationed at the United Nations. There were probably others.

Back up on the dock once again I hobbled to the stairs and up, then headed through the snowstorm, following the footsteps we had made coming out here.

There was a stretch of at least a hundred and fifty yards of woods between the dock and the house. By the time I had made it to the other side, my soaked trouser legs were frozen stiff and my hands were numb from the cold.

I stopped before I started across the yard to the back door, and looked up toward the house. At first I thought the swirling snow was playing tricks on my vision, but then I realized I was seeing flashing red lights. Somewhere near the front of the house. Flashing red lights.

I stumbled across the backyard, but instead of climbing the steps to the porch I went to the side of the house. From there I could see at least a half dozen police cars, their red lights flashing out front in the driveway.

What the hell had brought the cops out here? The only thing I could think of was Yushenko. He must have done something back in the city that brought them out here.

I turned and, keeping low, raced across the backyard and into the woods. In this wind, and the seas that would probably be storming out past Montauk Point, it would take two hours or more to make it to the twenty-mile rendezvous point. All it would take would be for one of the cops to come down to the dock, guess that a boat had been here, and call the Coast Guard.

I could not outrun a Coast Guard cutter, nor could I hide from their radar. And if the Coast Guard did come out after me, I was certain the Soviet trawler would not stop to pick me up, orders or no orders.

Back at the stairs I raced down to the dock and out to the boat. I climbed aboard and dashed to the pilot house, where I cracked the throttles and hit the starter buttons.

After several seconds of grinding, the big, low-speed diesels kicked into life one after the other and settled down to a gentle chugging.

Out on the deck I cast off the bow and stern lines, and almost immediately the big boat began slewing around, trying to get its nose into the northwest wind.

In the pilot house once more, I hauled the wheel all the way over to port, eased the gear lever into forward, and gentled the throttles so that the boat turned away from the dock out into Fort Pond Bay.

For a few seconds, as the boat was abeam of the wind, I was sure she was going to roll over on her side, but then the bow came around, head into the wind, and I slammed the throttles full forward.

The engines, although they ran slow, were well maintained. They delivered a high torque, and were evidently geared way up, because the boat shot ahead, slamming through the waves which rose as high as seven or eight feet.

What conditions would be like out in the open

ocean remained to be seen, but for now I was making good time, and I was content that I had at least a fighting chance of making my rendezvous with the Soviet trawler. Beyond that it was anyone's guess what would happen.

To the left of the steering station I found a chart of the entire Long Island Sound and its nearby bays and inlets, and after a moment or two of pinpointing my exact location, I went back to the helm and laid a course straight out of the bay that would take me in a wide circle of the Montauk Point Light. Once I made it past that point, which I figured would take at least another twenty minutes, I would be able to turn straight out, due east.

Once I had the course set, I locked the wheel down, and went below where I found a fire axe, a powerful electric lantern, and in one of the cabinets a bottle of vodka.

I left the fire axe by the main hatch but took the signal lantern and vodka back up to the pilot house with me where I tuned the VHF radio to the Coast Guard frequency, braced myself in the pilot's chair, and opened the vodka bottle.

I had the feeling that Yushenko's safe house was more than that. With this boat, the house was a perfect place for incoming agents to enter the country without having to go through the sham of being attached to the U.N. or the Soviet embassy in Washington.

It was too bad I had not been able to contact Hawk, but I figured there were going to be a great many other trade-offs before I actually got to Kobelev.

It was worth it though. If the man became head

of the entire KGB, the free world would suffer the grievous consequences. He had to be stopped. No matter what it took.

The vodka was mild and very smooth, and as the boat continued to plunge through the building seas I tried to clear my mind, to prepare myself for the confrontation that was going to happen, sooner or later, between me and the Puppet Master.

Eight

It had easily been three hours since I had cleared the Montauk Point Light. The wind had abated somewhat, and the snow had stopped—improving visibility—but the sky was still heavily overcast.

The big diesels turned over slowly, keeping the boat headed into the wind as I stood out near the bow with the signal lantern. I had sent three longs and one short toward all four points of the compass with no answer for the last half hour. I didn't think the trawler had left the vicinity, nor did I think I was so far off course that my signal was not visible. So why weren't they answering?

If I could not make contact this morning, I would have to make landfall farther down the coast, get to Baltimore or some other big city, come up with a passport, and fly to Germany. From there I could make my way across into the East Zone and turn myself in to the military authorities.

But all that would take time. Too much time. And with no guarantees and even less likelihood of success.

Hanging on to the handholds at the front of the pilot house I worked my way across to the port side, aimed the lantern straight out toward the east, and signaled again: three longs and one short. Three longs and one short.

A moment later a pinprick of light due east answered my signal. Three longs and one short.

I signaled again and received an answer. The tidal current here evidently was stronger than I'd figured it would be, and I had not come as far from shore as I'd thought.

I watched toward the east, cocking my head slightly so that I could listen better for the sounds of a ship's engines.

A few minutes later the signal came again, the light much stronger now. I signaled back and waited.

Within another five minutes I could definitely hear the throbbing of powerful engines, and I raised the signal lantern and once more sent the three longs and one short. Almost instantly the signal was sent back to me, the light now very strong, probably within a hundred yards of me. A moment later a spotlight shown directly on me as the trawler's engines slowed down.

The ship, flying the Canadian flag and outfitted as a commercial fisherman, appeared out of the darkness like some kind of apparition, circled around behind me, then came up parallel about twenty yards from port side.

Two crewmen stood amidships on the huge trawler which had to be at least a hundred feet long, and one of them swung an arm around and threw something.

A small, hard ball of rope, knotted around a piece of lead, thumped on deck and I scrambled aft, grabbed it, and started hauling in the thin nylon line it was attached to.

A hundred feet or so down the line, a pair of one-inch thick ropes were attached by a thick swivel hook. Once I had the double lines aboard, I looped them around a cleat on the rail, and started hauling on the top line. Immediately a bosun's chair jerked down the line from the trawler and within a couple of minutes I had it aboard.

I waved up at the two crewmen waiting to haul me up, then turned and hurried below decks. It was like a morgue down there, and for a moment I looked at Cynthia's body wrapped in my raincoat. When I got back we were going to have to find out who she was.

I pulled up the bilge hatch and then grabbed the fire axe from where I had laid it by the main hatch. The less questions that followed me, the easier it would be for me to sell myself to Kobelev, I figured. I did not want this boat with its gruesome cargo being discovered, and questions raised.

Swinging the axe with all my might, I drove the blade down into the shallow bilge, biting into the hull planking between a pair of cross braces.

I swung again, the wood beginning to chip away, and within a couple of minutes I had a small hole in the hull through which sea water began to trickle.

Within two more minutes the water pouring into the boat had risen above the bilge, over the sole, and was already ankle deep on me. It would take less than an hour for the boat to sink to the bottom, and she would probably never be found.

I threw the axe down, looked one last time at Cynthia's body, then scrambled topsides where, around the side of the pilot house, I strapped myself into the bosun's chair, swung out over the rail, and signaled for the crewmen aboard the trawler to haul me up.

Immediately the chair swung away from the boat —wildly because of the wind and the relative motions of the two ships—and I was on my way up to the trawler.

Halfway up the line, the big trawler rolled to starboard at the same time as the boat I had come out on rolled to port, and I was dumped for a second or two into the sea. Then the lines twanged taut, rocketing me upwards and slamming me violently from side to side. My head snapped back, and for a minute or two I was completely dazed. I felt strong hands pulling at me, hauling me over the rail, and someone was shouting at me, first in Russian and then in English.

"Where is Stanislav Antonovich?"

"He's dead," I mumbled, recovering my senses. "Dead!" I shouted. I sat up with the help of the two Russian seamen. "There is no one aboard, and she's sinking, release the lines!" I shouted.

"Stanislav is dead?" one of them asked in broken English.

"Yes, comrade," I said in Russian. "He is dead. I killed him. Now release the lines. That ship is sinking."

Both men looked with astonishment from me to the boat I had just left and back to me. One of them had a gun in his hand.

"Cut the line and I will take him to the captain," he said.

"Yes," the other one said, and the man holding the gun helped me to my feet and motioned me toward an open hatch.

I looked toward the boat that was already beginning to wallow in the heavy seas because of the water she had taken aboard, and shook my head. Then I turned and went down through the hatch.

Halfway down a narrow passageway that ran the width of the ship, we went through another hatch, up four steps and were on the bridge, illuminated only by a dim red glow and the green traces on a radar screen.

In addition to the helmsman, communications officer, and one other man (all dressed in Canadian uniforms) a huge man, who must have weighed at least three hundred pounds, stood by the forward windows. His legs were spread as he braced himself against the motion of the ship, and his hands were clasped behind his back.

"Here is the American, sir," the crewman who had brought me up snapped. "Stanislav Antonovich is dead."

The huge captain turned to face me. "So," he said. "What has happened then?"

"I killed him," I replied in Russian before the crewman behind me had a chance to speak. "And I killed Oleg Dmitrevich Yushenko as well as another of his bodyguards . . . a man named Mikhail . . . although unfortunately I did not have the time to catch his last name or patronymic."

The Russian I was speaking was grammatically correct and very formal. St. Petersburg Russian, it was called.

"Are you armed?" the captain asked. His voice was soft, but totally devoid of emotion, as were his eyes. Except for the slightly amused expression on his lips, his face could have been that of a robot's.

I slipped my stiletto from its sheath and

Stanislav's Magnum from my pocket and held them out to the captain. "Only these," I said. There were still traces of blood on the blade.

The captain stepped forward and took the weapons, looked at them for a moment, and then handed them to the crewman behind me.

"That will be all, Nikita," he said. His eyes flickered to me. "Is there anyone aboard your vessel to take her back?"

"No," I said. "But I put a hole in her hull. She will be sunk within the hour."

"Very good," he said. The crewman had backed away and left the bridge. The captain smiled. "I'm afraid you've given poor Nikita Andrevich quite a fright. He has never seen an American. You're his first. And when you pulled out your little knife with blood on it, he was convinced that all the stories he heard as a child were absolutely true."

"And what were those stories?" I asked.

The captain threw back his head and laughed. "Why, that you Americans are all cold-blooded murderers whose aim is to take over the world. I'm sure that when you pulled out your weapons, poor Nikita was certain you were going to take our ship singlehandedly. I'm rather surprised he didn't shoot you."

I smiled. "I am defecting, Comrade Captain. I want to offer my knife and my skills to Comrade Kobelev. If the world is to be dominated, let it be under Russian rule."

The captain slapped his leg with his right hand. "Hear, hear," he said. "Well said. And now you will be given quarters, a place to bathe, dry clothes, and you will join me for breakfast."

"My pleasure," I said.

The captain said something to one of his officers that I couldn't quite catch because he was speaking too quickly, and in what sounded like an Asian dialect.

"Sergei will show you to your quarters," he said to me in a more formal Russian.

I inclined my head and followed the officer off the bridge, then aft to a small cabin occupied by two young men.

"Leave," the officer said to the young men, both of whom jumped up immediately, without question, and scurried out of the room.

The man then turned to me, his tone and expression icy. "Anything you may require in these quarters, you may consider yours. The bath is there," he said indicating a narrow doorway in the aft bulkhead. "The captain usually has his breakfast at 0800 hours." He looked at his wristwatch. "That is in forty-five minutes. Please be ready. I will come for you."

"Thank you," I said, and the officer turned and left the cabin, closing the door behind him.

I waited a couple of minutes and then went to the door and eased it open a crack. The companionway was deserted, but what was more important to me at this moment, was that I had not been locked in. Although where I would go was a moot point.

When the officer returned for me forty-five minutes later, I was ready. I had stripped off my wet clothing, had taken a leisurely hot shower, shaved and then dressed in a pair of dungarees and a sweatshirt as well as clean white socks and deck shoes.

I followed the man back down the companionway, up the four steps and then through a hatch opposite the bridge, entering the officers' wardroom.

The room was small and furnished only with a table, around which were eight chairs, and a sideboard with glasses, an ice bucket, and several bottles of Russian vodka.

The captain was the only one in the dining room, and he was seated at the head of the table that was ladened with food.

When I came through the hatch he got ponderously to his feet and smiled. "Good morning," he said.

The officer who had escorted me up there withdrew and quietly closed the door behind him. I crossed the room and sat down at the opposite end of the table from the captain as he went over to the sideboard and plunked several ice cubes in a glass he then filled with vodka.

He handed it to me, then poured himself a glass of vodka, this time without ice. When he turned back he nodded.

"I believe you will find this to be a pleasant drink," he said. "Ice for you, as I believe all Americans drink their liquor."

I raised my glass in salute and drank deeply of the ultra-smooth and very mild liquor. A hell of a way to start a morning, I thought.

"So now," the captain said, going back to his chair and sitting down. "Eat, and we shall talk. I have been beside myself with curiosity since you came aboard as to why you killed Comrade Yushenko and his two people."

I took several slices of toast from a platter he

offered me, a dollop of caviar, some smoked salmon and a few pieces of melon and pineapple. Evidently the captain was not aware of the fact that Stanislav had worked for Kobelev, otherwise he would have been more interested in his death than Yushenko's. Either that or for some reason Stanislav had been lying.

Briefly I explained to the man what had happened from the moment I had first contacted Yushenko outside the United Nations building, including the fact that the New York City Police had found my briefcase containing the rest of the files I had intended passing over.

Next I went into detail about Cynthia Patterson, and finally about Stanislav himself, and his distrust of me.

Everything that had happened would probably come out anyway if I was interrogated under drugs, so I figured I might as well begin by telling the truth. I only hoped that the auto-hypnotic training Dr. Wells had put me through over the past six months would help cover me as a CIA Clandestine Operations officer.

"Stanislav was dead," I said. "I had planned on going back up to the house and getting Mikhail, who seemed to me like a very sensible sort, when he shot me."

"Shot you," the captain said. "Extraordinary. Would you like my medical officer to look at your wound?"

"It's only a scratch," I said. "Unfortunately I reacted automatically, picked up Stanislav Antonovich's weapon and shot Mikhail. Self-defense."

The captain was shaking his head. "I can well

understand what must have been running through your mind at that precise moment. Unfortunately, however, Mikhail Ivanovich was very close to Comrade Kobelev."

I was raising my glass to my lips, and my hand stopped in mid-air. "What?" I said.

An expression of misery crossed the captain's features. "Poor Mikhail," he said. "He was Comrade Kobelev's stepson, you see. His wife's son by a previous marriage. It is unfortunate. Nikolai Fedor put great stock in the boy."

"What was he doing with Yushenko in New York?"

The captain looked sharply at me. "An improper question," he snapped. "If you are truly who you represent yourself to be, and if you expect to work for us, you will of necessity learn to curb your tongue."

How far to push this man? Kobelev did not surround himself with meek, mild-mannered people. His most trusted people, like his plans, were bold.

"Perhaps it is you, Captain, who should learn to curb his tongue," I said, and I sipped at my vodka.

He fumed, and started to get to his feet, but I put my glass down, and waved him back. "Listen to me, and listen very closely, Comrade Captain. Until a few days ago I was a high-ranking officer with the Central Intelligence Agency. At great risk to my life I left my post after killing two men and bringing out a number of important case-planning files. I brought a sample of those files to that idiot Yushenko, and what did he do? He called the New York Police Department and turned me in."

My voice had risen, and I stood up now, leaning way forward, my fists on the table top.

"I've been chased, I've been shot at, I've damned near been run over by a subway train, and I've been surrounded by phenomenal idiots! And for what reason? Simply because I have wanted to come to work for the Soviet government."

I straightened up, picked up my glass and drained it, then went over to the sideboard where I dumped out the ice, and filled it with vodka.

When I turned back the captain was looking at me, a hint of new respect in his expression.

I came back to the table with the bottle and sat down. "The Soviet Union, Captain, is in desperate need of a lesson in recruitment techniques."

"You just may be a double agent," he said.

I laughed. "You're damned right I might be a double," I shouted. "But, and my dear Comrade Captain, this is a very large *but,* I just might be who I say I am. Think about that."

"I have," the captain said. "Which is the only reason you have not been shot and tossed overboard."

"Fine," I said. "Then we understand each other."

"It is not necessary," he said. He looked at his watch. "In a dozen hours or so you will be gone from my command. We will rendezvous with the nuclear submarine *Solotkin* at 2000 hours."

I'd figured something like that. "Until then, Captain, I would imagine you'd like to learn from me about America," I said.

He beamed. "You are an astute man," he said with relish.

It had been a fairly easy guess, not only from the comments he had made about the young crewman who had brought me up to the bridge in the first place, but from his general attitude.

"Let's begin with Chrysler," he said. "Your government is, in effect, subsidizing the huge corporation. Explain to me the difference between that and our own system of government-controlled industry."

I chuckled. In twelve hours we would rendezvous with a Soviet submarine. It was going to be a long twelve hours.

"A loan guarantee is hardly a controlling subsidy," I began.

Our "breakfast" lasted until a few minutes after one in the afternoon and, head buzzing from the vodka, I went back to my cabin where I lay down on my bunk and fell instantly into a deep sleep.

I dreamed again about Bob McKibbens and his wife and three children—all girls. What was disturbing about the dream was that I not only knew it was a dream, but knew such irrelevant disconnected details as the fact that McKibbens had always wanted a son, that in the fifties he was a Yankee fan, and that he had a fishing cabin on the remote west shore of Lake Winnepeg in Canada.

I woke once around four in the afternoon, and lay for a couple of minutes still half in my dream, listening to the sounds of the ship, and then fell asleep again.

What seemed like seconds later, the officer the captain had called Sergi was standing over my bunk, the cabin lights on.

"It is time," he said when I opened my eyes.

For a moment I forgot completely where I was, but then it all came back in a rush like water boiling over and I sat up with a start.

."We have made the rendezvous with the *Solotkin?*" I asked.

The officer stepped back. "The boat will be surfacing momentarily. The captain wants you transferred as quickly as possible."

"Troubles?" I asked, swinging my legs over the edge of the bed and sitting up. I fumbled around for the deck shoes, then put them on and tied the laces.

"I asked if there is any trouble," I said, looking up.

"We were overflown around 1400 hours, and again about an hour ago by an American Coast Guard Search and Rescue aircraft."

I got up. "How about a jacket, or a coat," I said.

The man looked at me for a long moment, mistrust and a bit of fear evident in his eyes, but then he nodded his head toward a locker. "In there."

I went across the cabin and opened the locker. Inside, hanging in neat rows, was the clothing of the two crewmen whose room I had been given. I grabbed a jacket and pulled it on. "Are we being radar-scanned?" I asked.

"No more questions," he said.

"Look, goddammit," I shouted, "either answer my questions or we'll call the captain down here and I'll ask him."

Real fear was evident in his eyes at the mention of the captain. "The aircraft scanned us. We're clean at the moment, however."

"Let's get going then," I snapped. "Our Coast Guard is damned efficient, and I'm sure they've got this vessel pegged as Soviet. No doubt they've informed our Navy, and you'll be having a visitor before too long."

We left the cabin and hurried down the corridor and out onto the deck.

The wind had calmed down considerably, but there was a thin fog that made visibility much beyond a hundred yards impossible in the dark.

Two other crewmen were on deck, as well, and they had a line and a bosun's chair ready for my transfer.

"STAND BY FOR SURFACING OFF THE STARBOARD SIDE," a voice blared in Russian over the ship's PA system.

The hatch we had just come through clanged open, and the captain came out onto the deck. The officer who had awakened me and the two crew members stiffened to attention.

"As you were," the big man bellowed, and he clapped me on the back. "You enjoyed your little nap?"

I laughed. "Tell me something, Captain," I said.

He inclined his head, and I noticed out of the corner of my eyes that the crewmen were listening.

"I told you everything about America, now tell me something about the Soviet Union. Does everyone drink vodka that early in the morning?"

The captain roared, tears coming to his eyes. "No," he sputtered. "No." He held his stomach as he laughed. "We would never get any work done. And if you should be indiscreet and mention to Comrade Kobelev that you spent half the day with me, drinking and talking, I surely will be keelhauled."

"Not to worry, Captain," I said. "You've been a most congenial host. Once I get settled, if there is anything I can do for you don't hesitate to ask."

This sent the man into another fit of laughter,

but at that moment the ship's siren began to sound, and we all turned to look over the rail as a huge, ominous black mass rose up out of the ocean, the numbers S7737 painted on the conning tower along with the letters C C C P. The *Solotkin*.

Within seconds four crewmen from the sub had scrambled up from a hatch and the trawler crewmen sent over the weighted line. The transfer line was hauled across the fifty yards or so of open water, and the bosun's chair made ready for me.

"I wish you much luck," the captain said, shaking my hand. "I sincerely do. Perhaps in a year or so, when you are settled in, and I am home on leave, we will have another breakfast."

"Perhaps," I said, and I stepped forward and let the crewmen strap me into the chair.

Nine

The captain of the Soviet nuclear submarine *Solotkin* was different from the trawler captain in almost every respect. Where the trawler captain was a huge man, the submarine commander was small, dapper, with gold wire-rimmed glasses. Where the trawler captain was loud and boisterous, the sub's captain was very quiet, a stern, pinched expression seemingly permanently affixed to his face.

Once I had been transferred, I had been immediately hustled below where I was escorted amidships to the command center just beneath the conning tower.

The boat had already submerged, and by the time I ducked through the hatch into the dimly lit room, we were already accelerating toward flank speed.

The captain stood at one end of the navigation table discussing something with a burly, dark-skinned officer. Besides those two, there were the helmsman at the aircraft-type controls, the communications officer, sonar and radar men, and an officer seated at what I took to be the boat's weapons control console.

No one looked up when I came through the hatch, but the crewman who had escorted me here from aft turned and left, closing the hatch behind him.

"Good evening, Captain," I said. I was standing at the far end of the room.

The captain looked up, no expression on his face, then barely nodded his head toward the officer he had been speaking with.

The big man came around the table to me, bringing his right hand up as if he wanted to shake. I started to raise my hand when without warning the man doubled up his fist and smashed it into my face.

It was like a pile driver. My head snapped back, the room spun, and I staggered backwards, momentarily dazed. In a second or two I had regained my balance and started toward the man, but a pistol appeared in his hand, and I stopped in midstride, the blood pounding in my ears.

"When you come in contact with any officer aboard this boat, you will snap to attention," the officer said in English.

"You have my invitation, you motherless pig, to lay your weapon aside," I said in perfect Russian. "Then we will discuss your treatment of me."

The man's jaw tightened, and his hand holding the weapon shook.

"Yurianovich," the captain said very softly.

The officer backed off, once more in perfect control of himself as the captain came around the table to within a foot or so of me.

He looked up at my hair, into my eyes, at my chest and down to my feet, then back up again to my eyes. "You are an insolent bastard without manners," the man said gently, almost as if he was speaking words of comfort to a child. "It appears that it will be up to us to teach you proper respect."

"Is this how you treat all high-ranking officers?" I snapped. "Friends of the Soviet Union? Comrade Kobelev's men?"

"The Komitet is not here at sea," the captain said, his voice still deadly calm. "Here, I am the commander, the officers aboard this vessel my representatives. I hope for your sake you remember that. We will be at sea at least four days."

"And on the fifth day I shall fully report this matter," I said. My instincts told me to keep my mouth shut, but I still had to play the part of the disgruntled CIA officer.

The captain shook his head. "It will be a long voyage for you," he said. Then he turned to the big officer. "Yurianovich, if you will be so good as to escort this man to his quarters?"

"Aye, aye, Captain," the officer said. He motioned toward the hatch with his pistol, but I didn't move.

"At great risk to my life I defected to your people in New York City," I said. "Why am I being treated this way?"

"If he gives you the slightest trouble," the captain said, ignoring me. "Shoot him. We'll eject his body from one of the torpedo tubes."

"Yes, sir," the officer said with relish.

The captain turned to me. "You are a traitor to your own country. At this moment you have no home, you have no rights. You are a non-person, and you shall be treated as such. What your disposition will be when we arrive at our destination is for others to decide. At this moment you are nothing more to me than a dangerous cargo."

I started to object, but the captain held up a hand for my silence.

"If you cause any trouble aboard this vessel, I will have you killed. It is as simple as that."

"I would suggest, Captain, that you communicate with Comrade Kobelev, before you do anything rash," I said, then turned and stepped through the hatch out into the passageway.

We went all the way aft, behind the engine room and down one deck, where the officer motioned me into a small storage room, with a single dim red light bulb encased in a stiff wire mesh overhead. The compartment was cold and damp and contained nothing other than a couple of wooden crates stacked up along one bulkhead.

Two other men joined us a moment later, one of them carrying a five foot length of chain with a heavy ring at one end and an old-fashioned leg iron at the other. The second man carried a bucket.

"Strip," Yurianovich said.

"Go to hell," I snapped, backing away from him. I dropped into a crouch and tensed my muscles.

The two crewmen laid their things on the deck at the officer's signal, and then came at me from opposite directions.

I lashed out with my left hand, smashing a karate blow to one crewmen's neck, and spun around, kicking out with my right foot, catching the other man in the groin.

Too late I caught a movement out of the corner of my eye as the officer came up behind me, and as I started to swivel back something very hard smashed into the back of my head, and the floor came up to meet my face.

I was vaguely conscious of hands grabbing at me, and then something cold and very hard at my ankle. But my first real sensation was of a bone-chilling cold that was overshadowed only by a throbbing headache.

I mentally explored my body, but as far as I could tell I was not badly injured. The compartment was quiet except for the hum of the engines, and after a while I opened my eyes.

The light was still on, but I was alone. I sat up. I was nude, my left ankle clamped in the leg iron which was attached by the chain to the bulkhead. The bucket was lying a few feet away.

If this was how I was going to have to travel, it was indeed going to be a long four days. And I wondered now just what my reception in the Soviet Union would be like if this was any example.

I got to my knees and then stood up, the compartment spinning for a moment, a wave of nausea washing over me. But it passed quickly, and I shuffled out to the limit of the short chain. To the left I could just reach the bucket, but to the center I was at least five feet away from the crates, and to the right that far again from the hatch.

The temperature in the compartment was no more than fifty or fifty-five degrees, and I tried to remember what I knew about hypothermia. The important thing would be food to provide enough calories for my body to generate heat. I would need water as well to avoid dehydration.

I didn't think they meant to kill me. If that was the case they would have done it when I was unconscious. They were softening me up for my interrogation once I got to Moscow. Which meant they were going to have to make sure I stayed alive long enough to get there.

The chain was held to the bulkhead and to the clamp on my ankle by two thick bolts, each with a double nut, impossible to undo without tools. Everytime I moved my leg the iron clamp bit into my ankle, chaffing the skin away.

Four days, I thought. I could either lay down and give in to the cold, letting the boat's doctor keep me alive. Or I could fight it.

"Sonofabitches," I said in English, and I got down on the deck and began doing push-ups, slowly, in a smooth rhythm one after the other.

I figured I would do a couple of hundred, and then rest as best I could for a couple of hours. Whenever the cold began to penetrate too deeply into my muscles I would do another set of two hundred. How long I could keep that up was another matter, but it was definitely better than simply giving in to them.

As I did my exercises I locked my mind on to Kobelev, one part of me wishing his death to be a particularly slow and painful one, yet another more rational part of myself contemplating a very quick, clean kill—and then escape.

About five minutes later, when I was nearing the two hundred mark, the hatch opened. I looked up as the officer called Yurianovich came in. He was carrying a tray of food and a cup of tea.

"Continue with what you're doing," he said from the doorway. "Make no sudden moves and I will leave this within reach."

I didn't say a thing, but continued with my push-ups. After a couple of seconds he came all the way into the compartment and set the food down and went back to the hatch.

One more push-up and I looked up as Yurianovich stepped back into the compartment with a bucket. For a second I had no idea what he was doing, but then he swung the bucket around, the handle in one hand, the bottom in the other, splashing ice water over my entire body.

The shock to my system was massive, causing my breath to catch in my throat and my heart to skip a beat.

"Manners," the man said. "You must learn your manners." He backed out of the doorway, and closed the hatch behind him.

I got slowly to my feet, shivering almost uncontrollably. I was thoroughly soaked, my muscles ached, and I was suddenly very tired. I had not slept or eaten in what seemed like days, and I knew it would not be very long before what little strength I had left would be gone.

I picked up the tray of food—a thin vegetable soup, a meaty stew, and a large hunk of dark bread —and took it and the tea to one side of the room. There I hunched down, my back against the cold bulkhead, and began to eat.

Manners, the man had said. As I ate I stared at the hatch, a deep hatred smoldering inside of me that gradually began to crystalize into a plan.

I felt much better after I'd finished eating, and most of my shivering was abated. With the tray I had been given a knife, fork, and spoon, all of them stamped out of thick, heavy metal.

I took the flat-bladed knife and crawled out to the middle of the compartment where a plate was set flush into the deck. It was held down by a dozen screws which I started to undo.

Manners, I kept thinking. Kobelev, of course, was now aware of my existence. He knew that I was aboard this vessel, and by now he possibly knew what had happened at the safe house. He knew therefore that I was not an ordinary defector. He would be interested, and it was up to me to keep his interest piqued enough so that he would eventually want to meet me face to face.

The first seven or eight screws came out easily, but then it took me at least half an hour to undo the others, the knife blade twisting nearly half off its handle.

When I was finally finished I pried the plate up from the recessed lip and laid it aside. A few inches beneath the opening were a half-dozen thick cables and a maze of piping. Part of the ship's electrical system and pressure hull plumbing no doubt. This was likely one of several hundred access points for maintenance.

I laid the knife down and turned around, so that my left leg was now over the opening. Steadying the iron clamp around my ankle with one hand and my foot with the other, I began hitting the nut holding the clamp together against the edge of the opening.

With each blow the edge of the leg iron bit into my skin. After a few minutes my foot was covered with blood, but the nut was beginning to loosen a tiny amount with each hit.

If someone came to investigate the tapping sound, I would be stopped, of course, but I was hoping that the small amount of noise I was making in this remote section of the ship would go unnoticed long enough for me to at least undo the bolt.

It took nearly half an hour to loosen the first nut enough to unscrew it with my fingers, and nearly forty-five minutes of work to loosen the second nut. The leg iron parted when I had them both off, and I tossed it aside and stood up.

My ankle was numb and covered with blood, but the cuts were mostly flayed skin, and so superficial that the blood stopped flowing almost immediately.

I went to the hatch and eased it open a crack. The companionway was deserted. About twenty feet away was a flight of metal-runged stairs leading up to the main deck.

Directly overhead was the after-hatch compartment. Forward was the engine room and aft was the torpedo room. I could hear some men talking above, but their voices were too muffled and faint for me to make out what they were saying.

Evidently no one had heard the noise I made loosening the nuts, because no alarm had been sounded. There was no way I would be able to make it topsides with any chance of success without a weapon. My only option now was to wait until the officer Yurianovich or one of the crewmen came back. Probably with another bucket of water to continue my softening-up treatment, I thought as I closed the hatch and turned back. But that could be hours from now, possibly not even until tomorrow morning.

I grabbed the access plate I had unscrewed from the deck and, using it as a pry bar, levered the cover off one of the wooden crates. The box contained a single piece of machinery that looked to me like a pump. A few moments later I had the second crate opened and it contained a similar piece of machinery.

Disappointed, I set the access plate aside. I don't know what I had expected to find in the crates, but I had hoped for something that would have been of more use to me as a weapon. Maybe a piece of pipe.

The pumps were sealed in thick plastic bags, and I was about to tear one of the bags open so that I could use the plastic as a blanket for warmth, when the hatch started to swing open.

I snapped around and leaped noiselessly across the compartment as Yurianovich came through the door. He was carrying another bucket of water.

"Manners . . ." he was saying, but the word died in his throat and his eyes opened wide in surprise.

I was on him in an instant, grabbing a handful of his shirt front and pulling him all the way into the compartment with one hand, slamming the hatch shut with the other.

The man dropped the bucket and started to grab for his gun when I turned on my heel and smashed the edge of my right hand into the bridge of his nose, which exploded in a mass of blood.

He rocked back on his heels as he started to raise his pistol. At the same moment I drove the heel of my hand upwards against the tip of his nose, driving the broken bone and cartilage into his brain.

His entire body convulsed and he crashed backwards, his head bouncing with a sickening thud off the unyielding deck plates. Then he was completely still.

I remained where I was crouched, holding my breath, listening for the sounds of an alarm. But none came, and after a few seconds I went to where Yurianovich lay and checked his pulse.

He was dead. Still another in this gruesome business.

Within five minutes I had stripped the body of its clothes and put them on myself. They were too large, and I had to roll up the shirt sleeves and trouser legs, but the warmth was a blessing.

Lastly, I grabbed the gun from his hand. It was a Makarov 9mm semi-automatic, one of the more expensive Soviet weapons. The clip was full and a shell was in the chamber.

Manners, the man had said. I hadn't wanted any trouble. At least not until I got to Kobelev himself. But if they wanted to create problems, I would do my damnedest to give them a run for their money. Kobelev would expect it.

I brought the hammer back to the safety position, went to the hatch, and opened it just a crack. The passageway was still deserted, and I slipped outside, closing and dogging the hatch behind me.

Silently I went down the companionway and started up the stairs. At the top, before I peeked up over the level of the deck, I stopped to listen. I could hear someone singing, somewhere forward; in the compartment directly overhead, there was silence.

Taking a deep breath, and letting it out silently, I eased myself upwards so that I could just look over the edge of the deck.

No one was in the compartment, although I could hear the singing from forward a little more distinctly now.

I scrambled all the way up and raced forward to the hatch, where I flattened myself against the bulkhead and carefully cocked the hammer of the Makarov all the way back.

"On the double, seaman," I snapped in Russian, careful to keep my voice low so only the man in the next compartment forward could hear me.

The singing stopped.

"Aft," I said urgently. "Move!"

"Aye, aye, sir," someone said, and a second later a young crewman stepped through the hatch. I raised the gun to the back of his head.

"Freeze or you die!" I whispered in Russian.

The crewman started to turn, but then felt the pressure of the gun at the back of his head, and his entire body went rigid.

We stood like that for a couple of seconds, until I was sure he had calmed down enough to listen to me.

"I'm going to take the gun away from your head in a moment and put it in my pocket," I said softly. "Do you understand what I am saying?"

The crewman started to nod his head, but then thought better of it. "Yes, sir," he said instead.

"If you do as I say you will live. If you make any sudden move or gesture, I will kill you. Do you understand that?"

"Yes, sir," the young man said with difficulty.

I carefully took the gun away from his head and put it in my pocket, keeping my finger on the trigger, then stepped back. "Turn around very slowly now, and then head forward to the Command Center. I'll be right behind you."

He hesitated a moment.

"I don't want to kill you, and I won't unless you force me into it," I snapped.

The crewman turned and headed forward through the engine room, past the crew's quarters and mess, and finally through the Missile Control Center. Others in the crew whom we encountered looked up in surprise as we passed, but they were well disciplined enough not to say a thing or to interfere.

When we got to within a few feet of the Command Center hatch, I told the crewman to stop.

Over his shoulder I could see the helmsman and sonar operator at their consoles. I only hoped that the captain was inside as well.

I stepped to one side. "You can return to your duty station now," I said softly.

The young man stiffened. "I can't let you go in there, sir," he said. He was very frightened.

"Then you will die and I will go in there anyway," I said. "I don't want to kill anyone, and I won't. Now return to your duty post."

The young man hesitated just a moment longer, then slowly turned, glanced back at me, and headed aft.

When he had gotten across the compartment and started through the aft hatch, I turned and ducked inside the Command Center, slammed the hatch shut and dogged it.

The captain was just coming through a hatch on the forward bulkhead across the compartment from me. I turned and pulled the gun out of my pocket.

"Good evening, Captain," I said in Russian.

The man stopped just inside the Command Center, and looked across the long compartment at me, no expression in his eyes. "Where is Yurianovich?" he asked.

The others in the compartment had looked up and were staring open-mouthed at me.

"Dead," I said. "But the man left me no choice. I am a defector to the Soviet Union, Comrade Captain. I will not be treated like an animal."

"I see," the man said. "Are you taking me and this vessel hostage?"

I shook my head. "No," I said. "I want your word that I will be given a warm, dry bunk for the rest of this voyage. If you want me in restraints I will not resist. I ask only to receive reasonable treatment."

"Agreed," the captain said without hesitation.

I stepped forward, and laid the gun on the navigation table, then stepped back. The captain came forward, picked up the gun, and pointed it at me.

"Deck officer," he snapped.

One of the officers who had been standing near the helm came forward. "Aye aye, sir."

"Call for an armed guard up here on the double. I want this man stripped and placed in leg irons again. This time weld the irons to his leg and to the bulkhead."

"You dirty bastard," I said taking a half step forward.

The man smiled. "As I said, the *Komitet* does not exist aboard this vessel while she is at sea."

Ten

Someone in another room screamed, the piercing shriek echoing down the wide corridor, and I jerked my head up, trying without much success to focus on my surroundings.

I was in a lot of pain, but it came at me from so many different places on my body that I could no longer localize any single injury. My tongue felt swollen to twice its size, my eyes had puffed nearly shut, and when I swallowed I could taste blood.

Very little of what had happened to me over the past four days or so was clear in my mind. I remember that I had fought with the crewmen who had rechained me to the bulkhead in the submarine's storage room, and I also remember that my ankle was badly burned when the leg iron was welded.

After that the hours seemed to run together, the events indistinct, like kaleidoscopic images. I remember the ice water, and someone with a wet bath towel hitting me in my naked groin; and something happening with a soldering iron in my nostrils.

I also had a very vague recollection of walking barefoot across a dock at night. It was snowing, and I was being stuffed into the back of a van.

A face swam in front of my eyes, and I tried to see who it was, but the bright lights behind him formed a halo around his head, nearly blinding me.

"Robert McKibbens," the face said. "Do you know him?"

I tried to speak, but could not form any words.

"It's all right, Nicholas," the face said. "You may nod your head for a yes. Bob McKibbens, do you know him? Have you worked for him?"

I managed to nod my head, but it seemed to take every ounce of my strength.

Something was clamped to my penis and my gut involuntarily tightened.

"Bob McKibbens, is he really your boss?" the face said.

I nodded and at the same instant an unbelievably strong pain grabbed at me, as if my testicles had been placed in a vice, and I could hear myself screaming.

"Bob McKibbens, is he your boss?" the face said.

I was still screaming, the pain went on and on, and yet I was nodding my head, banging it against the seat-rest behind me. Yes, the answer screamed in my brain. Yes! I could see Bob's house. I could see his wife and daughters. Bob and I had played golf together. No handicap. Five bucks a stroke. Why wouldn't he listen?

"It's all right now," the face said, its voice soothing, and the pain was gone.

Bob McKibbens, I thought. A couple of years ago he had burned his hand when I knocked over a hot cup of coffee in the Company commissary down at Langley. I felt really bad about it, and in fact still felt bad about it.

"What did he say to you about it?" the soothing voice was asking.

Bob had been nice. It was an accident, he said, nothing more. But he had joked that having coffee with me was the most dangerous thing he had ever done for the Company.

"Tell me about Bob," the face was asking. Somehow I was lying on my back now, and I had the impression I was in a bed with wheels and being pushed down a corridor. The lights weren't so bright anymore.

What was there to tell about McKibbens? He had made his debut in North Korea. *Night Fighter,* they had called him, because of his intelligence work behind enemy lines. And then there had been that thing in Chile, and our network operations, as well as the entire East German thing. Christ, that had been a sweet set-up from Day One. No one had tumbled to that one, not even Senator Edwards during the big Congressional shakeup.

God, it was beautiful. Bob was like a great big wonderful octopus atop a mountain with eyes in the back of his head so that he knew what was going on around him every moment of the day. If he was a violinist, the joke had gone, he would have played the entire symphony himself.

The face laughed at the little joke just as the Company wags had laughed at it. But there was respect. Always respect for Bob.

The lights faded, and for what seemed like days I was drifting, comfortable now, no pain, just a gentle warmth in my left arm above the elbow. And it was pleasant to recall the old days with McKibbens and his *Raiders* until that sonofabitch Petullio down in Miami.

"Touchy," Bob had warned me. "Don't blow it Nick. Whatever the hell you do, don't blow it, just get the job done."

Juan Petullio, the little bastard. He wouldn't stand still, and killing him had been nothing more than an accident. An accident, Bob, for Christ's sake, can't you see it?

No, the dirty bastards. They could not see it. All those years down the drain. All those years it had taken me to finally see just what kind of an opportunist bastard McKibbens had been.

I was awake. Suddenly, and with more clarity than I thought was possible, I was seeing, and hearing and feeling again.

Someone helped me sit up and bring my legs over the edge of the hospital bed I was lying on.

I was in some kind of dispensary ward that contained half a dozen beds, some medical equipment along one wall, and a wide door that led out into a stone corridor.

A man in a white coat stood next to me, holding me steady. I turned to him and smiled.

"It's not necessary," I said, my voice surprisingly clear and steady. "I'm all right now."

"Are you sure?" the man said.

I nodded. "Can I have a cigarette?"

"I don't know . . ." the doctor started to say, when another voice—one I recognized—interrupted.

"Of course he can."

I turned my head to the left as a short man in a Soviet Army uniform, colonel's tabs on his shoulders, his boots polished to a high sheen, came across the room to me. He was smiling, and he handed a cigarette to me, then a light.

I inhaled deeply, the smoke making me a bit lightheaded. But I felt wonderful.

"How do you feel?" he asked.

I returned his smile. "Disconnected, but good," I said. I glanced around the room. "The Center, or Lubyanka Prison?"

"Lubyanka, actually," the colonel said. "The Center is next door."

"How long have I been here?" I asked, looking back at the man.

"Twenty-four hours," he said.

I knew that answer should have been surprising to me; it seemed like I had been here all of my life. And yet it didn't seem to faze me. Drugs? One part of my mind asked the question, while another part of me didn't really care.

"Can you walk?" the colonel asked.

"I think so," I said. I jumped down off the bed before either the colonel or the doctor could make a move to help me, and after just a split second of dizziness, I got my balance. My legs felt weak, as if I had been sick and had lain in bed for weeks, but other than that I felt fine.

The colonel took my arm and together we headed out of the dispensary and down the long, wide corridor.

"We had quite a long talk, you and I, while you were out," the colonel said conversationally. "Do you remember any of it?"

"Bits and pieces," I said. "Drugs?"

"A little electric shock treatment, and then some drugs. You were—how can I put it—almost too co-operative. Made us all a little nervous, you know."

"As I told Yushenko and then Stanislav An-

tonovich, I am defecting. I came over because I
want to work for Comrade Kobelev. Has he been
informed of my arrival?"

"Yes he has," the colonel said. "But you know,
Nicholas, we find it very difficult to believe some of
the things you told us. Especially about Bob
McKibbens and his East German work."

I almost asked him who the hell Bob McKibbens
was, but something made me hold back.

"You were about to say?" the colonel prompted.

I looked at him and shook my head. "Nothing,"
I said. "I was just wondering if you have me on a
tranquilizer now."

"Yes we do. That and a painkiller. We thought it
would be best."

"Best for whom or what?" I asked.

"A tribunal was held, Nicholas. You were found
guilty."

"Of what?"

"Of attempting to act as a double agent for the
United States. Your execution has been ordered.
As a matter of fact the firing squad is waiting out-
side at this moment."

"I see," I said, not understanding at all why I
was so calm.

"Any last words? Anything you'd like to tell me?
Anything at all?"

"Thanks for the cigarette," I said.

The colonel seemed disappointed, but then
waved it off. "Nothing," he said.

At the end of the long corridor we took a set of
wide stone stairs up two levels, then went through
a thick steel door out into a wide courtyard.

A canvas-covered truck was backed up near a
tall cement wall across the yard from the building,

and we headed arm in arm across to it.

"If there was anything . . . anything at all you might be able to tell me . . . I might be able to help reduce your sentence," the colonel said. "Perhaps to life imprisonment. Sooner or later there are always prisoner exchanges, and probably within a year or two you would be sent home."

Who the hell was Bob McKibbens, one part of my mind was asking, while another part of me understood that I would have to keep my mouth shut now at *all* costs.

It was snowing, and I was wearing nothing more than thin hospital pajamas, a robe, and slippers. Halfway across the courtyard a second lieutenant came out to meet us with an army greatcoat devoid of buttons or insignia.

"You must be cold. Would you like a coat?" the colonel asked.

"No, thank you," I said. "How about another cigarette?"

"Of course," the man said. We stopped and he produced another cigarette for me. This time I noticed it was an American brand. A Marlboro. He lit it for me, and we continued across the courtyard, where I was positioned by the wall.

"Normally we would bind you, hand and foot, and then place a black cloth sack over your head. But I'll leave it up to you."

"This will be fine," I said. "But you are making a mistake, Colonel."

"Yes?" he said stepping a little closer to me. About fifteen yards away the back of the truck was open. The lieutenant stood to one side, and on the tailgate a machine gun was set up, manned by two soldiers.

I looked into the colonel's eyes. "I defected to be with Comrade Kobelev, not to act as a double agent for the United States. You are wasting a valuable man."

"I sincerely wish we could believe that Nicholas."

He turned and stalked off across the courtyard back toward the building, never looking back.

I brought the cigarette up to my lips and drew the smoke deeply into my lungs. The mission had failed. I had done my damnedest to make it work, but with Kobelev's upcoming promotion to head of the KGB, he and the people around him had to be very cautious. Kobelev had to be protected. We had mounted this mission too late. It was as simple as that.

"Ready!" the lieutenant shouted.

I squared my shoulders and looked directly at the machine gun.

"Aim and lock!" the lieutenant shouted. The ejection slide on the machine gun was released with a loud snap.

"Damn," I said, half aloud. I took a deep breath, held it, and slowly closed my eyes.

"Fire!" the lieutenant shouted, and almost simultaneously someone else shouted, "Wait!"

A split second later the machine gun fired a burst that went wide, to the right of me, spattering the cement wall.

My knees went weak and I nearly fell to the ground, but I steadied myself after a moment and opened my eyes.

A bull of a man, moderately short and dressed in plain dark trousers, a gray tunic reminiscent of the one Stalin used to wear, and a fur coat open down the front, came across the courtyard. I would have recognized him any time, under any conditions.

"I'm glad I was on time," he said reaching me. His voice was rich, and deep, and there was a glint in his wide, dark eyes. His hair, what little I could see of it jutting out from beneath his fur cap, was platinum white.

He stuck out his hand. "Welcome to the Soviet Union, Nick Carter."

I shook his hand, his grip firm. "I'm happy to finally meet you Comrade Kobelev," I said. "Very happy."

He threw back his head and laughed, then glanced back at the lieutenant and two soldiers who were standing at ramrod attention. "I'm sure you are," he said.

He took my arm and together we went across the courtyard and out a side gate, the guards there snapping to attention as we passed, and then climbed into the back seat of a Zil limousine.

As soon as we had settled in, the driver took off through the city at high-speed. The streets were deserted and only a few scattered lights were still on. It was quite the contrast from New York City.

"What time is it?" I asked.

"After two," Kobelev said. We were speaking in Russian, and he switched to English, his pronunciation perfect, with only a slight British cast. "Would you be more comfortable in English?"

"It's of no matter," I said in St. Petersburg Russian, and Kobelev smiled.

"Very well," he said switching back to his native tongue. "Tell me again about poor Mikhail Ivanovich."

I looked at him, and, despite the darkness of the

car's interior, I could see genuine sadness in his eyes. "I'm sorry," I said. "But I didn't have much of a choice. I was defending my life."

"It amazes me. Mikhail was a better shot than that. I trained him myself, and of course he went to Academy Number One. You should be dead."

"The conditions were bad," I said. "And, looking back on it, I have the feeling now that he may have only been trying to wound me."

Kobelev shook his head. "He was doing what he thought was his proper duty. He gave his life in service to his country. It's as it should be."

We rode for a while then in silence, passing a large museum on the left, and then a sports stadium of some sort. A sign that read FRUNZE CENTRAL AIRFIELD flashed by, and the driver sped up.

For a time I considered killing Kobelev this morning, but then dismissed it. I was in a weakened condition, and was not at all sure I could manage Kobelev, who looked exceedingly strong, let alone his burly driver.

In addition, we were probably expected at the dacha, and there was a possibility we were being followed at this moment. I could not, however, turn around to take a look.

It took everything within my power to be pleasant to the man. Now that I had come this far, I wanted to get it over with.

Patience, I told myself. I would need patience.

"You know, Nicholas, my people do not trust you, nor do I. You're just too good to be true. Your story is just too pat."

"I came here to work for you, Comrade," I said. "Put me to work."

Kobelev smiled and nodded. "I will, indeed I will," he said. "But first we will have to fatten you up. You'll need food and exercise, and I'll have my personal physician attend to your wounds. Are you in any pain at the moment?"

I shook my head. "I believe I was given a tranquilizer and something for the pain."

"A couple of weeks rest, then, and you'll be fit."

"No," I snapped. "My wounds are superficial. I want to get started immediately. I came here to work, not to have a holiday."

Kobelev laughed out loud. "Work," he said. "From torture to the firing squad, and now he wants work. Rich. Very rich, Nicholas."

"Some men have their women, some their hobbies, for me there is work," I said. "Nothing else has any meaning."

"So it would appear," he said thoughtfully. "Are you telling me that you are another Stanislav Antonovich?"

"He was a dangerous man, Comrade, but not because he was an efficient killer, but because he was stupid. He had no finesse. No grace."

"You have?"

"Put me to work . . ." I started to say, but then I changed my mind. "Yes I do, and I think you know it."

A dangerous edge crept into his voice. "You refer to the incident aboard the *Akai Maru?*"

I nodded. "A brilliant plan, Comrade, that contained only one fatal error."

"Which was?" he barked.

"I was your enemy!"

"Very rich," he said slowly after a moment or two of silence. He turned and looked out his window at the passing scenery. We had left the city behind and the road cut through a thin birch forest. The snow had all but stopped, and the countryside seemed cold, lonely, and very desolate.

"It's pretty here in the summertime, except for the mosquitoes," Kobelev said, almost as if he had read my mind. He turned to me. "You will be staying at my country home. It is well guarded, so you will have no chance of escape. I must return to the city yet this morning, but I will be back later in the day, after you have had a chance to rest. We can talk then at much greater length." He seemed to think for a moment. "If it is work you desire, I have a little assignment for you. In Istanbul. Perhaps you would be interested?"

"Very," I said, suppressing a smile. Hawk had been correct. I had been interrogated, Kobelev had then met with me, and soon I would be sent out on a test mission. From that moment on I would be given more and more trust, and therefore increasing freedom.

There would come a time, very soon I hoped, that I would be able to take care of Kobelev finally, and then make my escape.

The driver slowed down, and we turned off the main highway onto a narrow dirt road. It wound its way deep into the woods, finally ending at a huge, ornately constructed house that looked to be at least two hundred years old.

Once the car was stopped, the driver jumped out and opened the back door for Kobelev. I followed a moment later, and the two of us went up the walk and entered the house by the front door. It opened into a narrow vestibule furnished with a coat rack, alongside of which was a mirror.

I looked at my image. There were no wounds visible on my face, but my eyes looked puffy and red-rimmed from the ordeal I had gone through. And my nose was tender from burns in my nostrils.

Kobelev was watching me, and I turned to him. "Do you give rewards for good service, Comrade?" I asked.

Kobelev nodded.

"When I return from Istanbul I would like a reward."

"Yes?"

"I want the Captain of the *Solotkin*. I won't kill him, I just want him for about an hour."

Kobelev chuckled. "I'll consider it," he said. We went across the vestibule and through a door with a carved, frosted-glass pane into the main entry hall of the house. A young, beautiful woman dressed in a thick velvet bathrobe, her feet bare, was just coming down the wide stairs.

"Papa," she said as we came in, and she skipped the rest of the way down, pecked him on the cheek, and then looked at me, frank curiosity in her wide, dark eyes.

"Nicholas, I'd like you to meet my headstrong daughter, Tatiana, who at this hour should be in bed asleep."

She laughed and extended her hand to me. "You must be the American my father has spoken of."

I took her hand, which was warm and very soft. "I'm very pleased to meet you," I said.

"And his Russian is gorgeous," she said lightly. "Although I don't care for his wardrobe."

"Back to your room now," Kobelev snapped.

"I'm not tired," she said.

Kobelev said nothing, and after a moment the

girl turned and went back up the stairs. For just an instant something had come into her eyes when she looked at her father. Had she been anyone other than Kobelev's daughter, I would have guessed it was hate.

But I soon dismissed the thought. Kobelev escorted me to my room upstairs, where I was examined soon after by his doctor, a young army major, and then put to bed, where I drifted almost immediately off to sleep.

Eleven

I don't think I had been asleep for more than a couple of hours when I awoke, aware somehow that someone had come into the room. I opened my eyes.

In the dim light that filtered through the windows from outside, I could see Kobelev's daughter Tatiana standing by the doorway.

I was about to ask her what she was doing in my room, when she untied her robe and let it fall off her shoulders to the floor. She was nude, her hair done up in the back. Her body was lovely, her breasts small, nipples erect, her stomach flat, and the small swatch of pubic hair a light brown.

She glided across the floor, threw the covers back and climbed into bed with me.

"Your father would probably have us both shot if he knew you were here," I said softly.

She laughed, the sound low and sensuous, and she placed a finger on my lips. "Say nothing," she said. "Papa went back to Moscow and everyone else is asleep."

She came into my arms then, her body incredibly soft, and almost immediately I could feel myself responding as she moved against me and let her hands begin to explore.

"Are you in pain Nicholas?" she asked, kissing my cheek and then behind my ear.

"Not now," I said. This was exceedingly foolish and very dangerous, but the entire mission had been filled with high risks. Another wouldn't make much difference, and besides, I have never been able to resist a beautiful woman for very long even under normal conditions. This morning I was even more vulnerable after the ordeal I had gone through with my interrogation and the firing squad.

For the moment then I forgot about my mission and Kobelev, as Tatiana gently pushed me over on my back and began kissing my neck, then my chest and belly, making little moaning sounds as she worked.

What information we had on Kobelev's family indicated that his wife and daughter had been insulated out here at the dacha for a very long time. It was a safe bet, however, that Tatiana had not spent that time knitting. She definitely knew what she was doing.

She straddled me finally and as we made love I reached up and carressed her breasts, then slid my hands down her sides to her hips and helped her thrust deeper and deeper.

When we were finished, she eased down on top of me, and kissed my lips.

"They didn't hurt you too badly," she cooed. "I'm glad."

I reached up and brushed a loose strand of hair away from her eyes. "Can you tell me something, Tatiana?" I asked gently.

"Mmmm?" she replied sleepily.

"Why is it you don't like your father?"

She stiffened in my arms, then pushed herself up and got out of bed, going immediately to fetch her robe and then pulled it on.

"I saw the look in your eyes before when your father told you to go to bed," I said, sitting up.

She looked at me, her face blank, then turned, opened the door and, slipping silently out into the corridor, was gone.

For a few moments I stared after her, wondering if I had made a huge mistake by mentioning her father. What I didn't need at this point was a strong enemy here in the house. One word from her, and I was reasonably certain that Kobelev would kill me himself.

I lay back on the bed finally, pulled the covers up, and closed my eyes. There were only six days left before the Presidium was scheduled to meet and consider Kobelev's promotion.

Six days, I thought as I drifted off to sleep again. Six days in which to convince Kobelev completely that I was sincere, plan for my escape, and then kill him.

The sun was streaming through the windows when I awoke again. Something cold was pressing against my bare chest. I opened my eyes and looked up into the face of the army doctor who had examined me this morning when I had come in. He was holding a stethoscope to my chest.

"Will I live?" I asked in Russian.

The young doctor smiled. "That depends upon how good you are with an épée or foil," he said. "Take a deep breath, hold it a second, and then let it out slowly."

I did as he requested.

"Again," he said, shifting the stethoscope.

Again I complied. When he was finished he straightened up and looked thoughtfully down at me for a moment.

"You've had quite an active life, it would appear," he said.

I smiled. "I hate television," I said.

A look of confusion crossed his face. "I'm sorry, I don't quite understand."

"No matter, Comrade Doctor, it is a bad American joke. Am I fit?"

"Amazingly so for what I have been told you were put through," the doctor said. He turned away and stuffed the stethoscope in his bag, which he snapped shut and then picked up.

"You mentioned something about an épée. Fencing?" I asked.

The doctor nodded. "Comrade Kobelev will be back at any moment. He called earlier to ask how you were doing, and if you would be fit enough for some exercise."

"And?"

The doctor shook his head in wonderment. "Aside from the burns in your nostrils, a few bruises here and there, and the cuts, scrapes, and burns on your ankle, you're fit. How do you feel?"

"Sore," I said sitting up and swinging my legs over the edge of the bed. The room was large, and near the window was a tall padded table with a clean white sheet draped over it.

The doctor motioned toward it. "Get up on the table. I'll send the masseur in for you."

"Tell him to be careful with me. I really am sore."

The doctor grinned. "I can't tell him a thing. He's deaf and blind."

"Wonderful," I said. I went around the bed and climbed up on the table as the doctor left the room and a moment later the door opened again.

I turned around as the largest man I have ever seen in my life ducked to come through the doorway. He was wearing sweatpants and a sleeveless T-shirt, his biceps almost as big around as my waist.

He had several clean white towels drapped over his shoulder and was carrying a tray which held various bottles of oil and rubbing alcohol.

I sat up and started to get down off the table, but he had come unerringly across the room, and with his left hand—that had to be six inches or more across at the palm—gently took my arm and guided me back on my stomach.

One twitch, one wrong move, and I figured this giant of a man could break me in two. I began to sweat as I lay perfectly still while he got ready.

He had set the tray and towels aside, and squirted some oil in his palms. I stiffened as he turned back to me and reached out for my neck and shoulders with those huge hands of his. If it got too bad I would roll away from him off the table and get out of there. I hadn't come this far to be killed or maimed by a clumsy masseur who didn't know his own strength and couldn't see what he was doing.

After a few exploratory touches to determine just how I was lying, he began his work, and it was wonderful. His touch was as gentle as a woman's and yet firm, with the feeling of tremendous power behind his fingers.

Soon I found myself relaxing, totally leaving my muscles in this amazing man's care. Slowly, but with finesse, he worked the knots and tightness out of my shoulders and arms, and even the individual joints of my fingers, before he started down my back. Whenever he neared a tender spot on my body from where I had been beaten, he instinctively changed his technique, so that not once did I feel even the slightest amount of pain.

For half an hour he worked on my back, lulling me nearly to sleep. Then he turned me over, as gently as a mother would turn her baby, and began on my chest.

Kobelev came in a few minutes later, and the giant stopped what he was doing and turned toward the door.

"I see you're in good hands, Nicholas," Kobelev said, coming across the room. He touched the masseur on the chest, and the big man turned back to me and continued his work. "How do you feel now that you've rested?"

"Much better," I said. There was something disturbing in his eyes. I wondered if Tatiana had said something to him about last night. If she had he was holding it well.

He looked at his watch. "It's not quite five now. We'll have dinner around eight, which gives us plenty of time for some exercise . . . that is if you're up to it."

"After this one finishes with me, I'll be up for anything," I said.

"Very good," Kobolev replied. "Clothing will be brought for you. When you are dressed, come downstairs; someone will direct you to the gym." He turned and went to the door, but then turned back before he left the room. "We'll discuss your first assignment this evening after dinner."

"Istanbul?" I asked.

"Yes," he said glancing back at me. "Tomorrow, if you're ready for it."

"I'll be ready."

"We'll see," he said, and left the room.

Once I got to Istanbul I was somehow going to have to get a message off to Hawk. Whatever Kobelev had in mind for me, it would not be pleasant. I just didn't want anyone to get hurt, and yet I had to prove myself.

Twenty minutes later the masseur had finished with me, and as he gathered up his bottles and towels, I patted him on the shoulder. He turned his sightless eyes toward me and grinned, then left the room.

As I was climbing down off the table the army doctor came back. He was carrying some clothing and other items which he laid on the bed.

"You look a lot better now than you did an hour ago," he said.

"I feel a lot better," I said. "The man is amazing."

"Yes."

"You didn't happen to bring any cigarettes with you?"

"On the bed," he said.

I looked through the items he had brought me, which included a couple of packs of Marlboros, a cigarette case and lighter, and an Omega chronometer with a stainless steel case and band.

After I had lit myself a cigarette, I quickly got dressed in clean underwear and socks, a pullover sweater, slacks, and a pair of light but sturdy shoes.

Everything fit perfectly.

"The transformation of man from beast to homo sapien," the doctor said. "If you're ready I'll show you to the gym."

"You don't approve of Comrade Kobelev's exercises?" I asked, following him out of the room.

He looked sharply at me. "That, Mr. Carter, is a very dangerous question to ask. Especially now."

"Now?" I asked as we went down the corridor and then headed down the stairs.

"He requested my presence in the gym," the doctor said in a low voice. "In case you should be injured."

"I see," I said. There were a number of things Nikolai Fedor did not know about me, however, among them the fact that I had been an inter-collegiate fencing champion four years in a row. Admittedly, that had been a number of years ago, but I still exercised regularly, and every time I was at AXE's Rest and Recuperation Ranch near Phoenix, I fenced with the facility director, who in his youth had been a world-class champion.

Kobelev was good; there was no doubt of that from what our records indicated. But I was not an amateur by any means, nor did I think he meant to kill me—not yet, and no matter what his daughter might have told him.

The gym was housed in a huge, high-ceilinged room at the back of the house, and was completely equipped with almost every kind of exercise equipment imaginable.

A set of stairs along one wall led to a second-floor observation deck where Tatiana was seated with another stunning woman whom I took to be her mother. She was a slightly older rendition of her daughter, and if anything was even more beautiful.

Kobelev wasn't here yet, but his wife leaned forward in her chair. "Nikolai will be here momentarily," she called down to us. Her voice was soft, with a slight European accent.

"Very good, Madam Kobelev," the doctor said. "May I present the American, Nicholas Carter."

She nodded her head gracefully.

"Madam Kobelev," I said.

"Please," she replied, a smile on her full lips. "You may call me Katrina Fedorovich." Tatiana had a very cold expression on her face. It looked as if she were pouting.

"A lovely name for an even lovelier lady," I said.

"Well spoken," Kobelev said coming into the gym.

The doctor and I both swiveled around. Kobelev was still wearing his suit. He took off his jacket and tossed it aside, then loosened his tie as he went across the gym to a locked wooden cabinet against one wall.

He opened the cabinet and from inside withdrew a pair of fencing foils, then turned and tossed one to me. I caught it by the shaft.

The tip guard was gone, the foil sharpened to a fine point. It was a killing weapon.

"In street clothes?" I asked.

"Why not?" Kobelev said with relish.

The doctor, absolutely no expression on his face, turned away from me, went up the stairs, and sat down behind the two women.

I looked up. Kobelev's wife seemed somewhat concerned, but Tatiana looked like a little girl moments before the first act of circus was to begin.

"Have you fenced before, Nicholas?" Kobelev called from across the gym.

I turned to him and grinned. "I'm familiar with the rudiments of the sport," I said.

I met him at the center of the floor, and brought the foil up to the *en garde* position. He did the same, a smile on his lips, and we both brought our left hands up and out, crossed foils, and the match began.

Kobelev's first parries, *ripostes* and *coups des temps* were guarded and somewhat weak. No doubt he was feeling me out and I played along with him, making my movements jerky and amateurish.

His first major bid for a quick kill came a split second after I had aimed a direct thrust, when he came with a lightning counter-attack in the form of the *coupe d'arrêt*. I had seen the tightening in his jaw muscles and the narrowing of his eyes, however, and I managed a feint and then a *disengagement*.

He was off balance for just an instant at that moment, so that when my straight thrust came after my change in direction, he was totally off guard.

The tip of my blade ripped his shirt, penetrating the skin slightly and drawing a small drop of blood.

I immediately backed off, bringing my sword up to the *en garde* position.

Kobelev stood flatfooted as he glanced down at his small wound and then back up at me, amazement and a touch of respect in his eyes.

Slowly he brought his sword up. "Why didn't you kill me when you had the chance," he asked, his voice very soft.

"I came here to work for you, Comrade, not to kill you."

He nodded, then glanced up at his wife and daughter. I followed his gaze, but it had been a ploy, and I snapped back at the same moment Kobelev hurled his foil at me like a spear. I just managed to step aside and bring my own foil up and around, deflecting his blade.

Totally defenseless now, Kobelev turned and raced toward the open cabinet, which contained several other blades, but I got to him first, bringing the tip of my foil up against his back, directly behind his heart.

One quick thrust and I would have penetrated his lung as well as his heart. He would have died instantly. And I would have been executed within hours.

"Do not reach for the blade, Comrade," I said. "The duel is over."

Kobelev stood stock still. "Do you mean to kill me?"

I backed off, once again bringing the foil up to the *en garde* position. And then, as he turned around to face me, I offered it to him shaft first. "As I have told you, I have come to offer you my services."

He carefully took the blade from me, and I let my hands drop to my sides. He inspected the tip, which was red with his own blood, then raised it so that it was less than an inch from my chest, just over my heart.

I looked directly into his eyes, and I could see the debate raging inside of him. Kill me or trust me?

After a long time, Kobelev finally backed off and tossed the foil aside. He then stepped forward, grabbed me by the shoulders, and kissed me full on the lips, the Russian form of deep affection and respect between two males.

"Welcome to the Soviet Union, Nick Carter. I have long needed a man like you."

"Thank you, Comrade," I said. "You'll not live to regret it."

An instant look of uncertainty crossed Kobelev's features, and I cursed my stupid tongue, but then he laughed.

"I don't expect I will," he boomed. "But I will die in my bed."

He clapped me on the back. "Come," he said, totally ignoring his wife, daughter, and the doctor up on the observation level, "we'll have a drink together before we clean up for dinner. I want to talk to you about Istanbul."

We left the gym, strolled down the corridor to the front of the house, and then to the right of the main staircase and entered Kobelev's study. Like every other room I had seen in this house, it was large and very well appointed. It didn't say much for the Soviet boast of a classless society.

Kobelev motioned me toward one of two deep leather chairs in front of the fireplace. As I went across the room and sat down, he went to a sideboard in one of the floor-to-ceiling bookcases.

A pleasant fire was burning on the grate, and the room was warm.

"Vodka?" Kobelev asked.

"Cognac if you have it," I said. "To tell the truth I hate vodka."

Kobelev laughed. "Rich," he said. "You'll make a poor Russian unless you develop a taste for our national drink. But, cognac it is for now."

He poured the drinks, came back across the room and handed me mine, then sat down.

For a minute or two we sat sipping our drinks as we stared into the fire, but then Kobelev turned toward me.

"What do you know about Istanbul?"

"I've been there a couple of times for the Company," I said. "It's a big, dirty city and the Turks are suspicious of everyone."

"Are you known there?"

"In some circles."

Kobelev seemed to contemplate my answer for a moment, and he took another sip of his vodka. "Does the name Larry Tripp mean anything to you?"

It did, but for a moment I couldn't quite put my finger on it.

"British," Kobelev prompted. Then I had it.

"Of course," I said. "I met him once maybe seven or eight years ago in London. I think he was posted as head of station in Istanbul a short time after that."

Kobelev was nodding. "Exactly. He's still there."

"I would have thought by now he should have been promoted out of that hell-hole."

"On the contrary, he'd probably stay there until retirement if we left him alone."

The room was suddenly cold. He continued.

"Mr. Tripp, it seems, has a rather unfortunate penchant for gambling. At this moment he's rather heavily in debt."

"It would ruin him if it got out," I said, suspecting what was coming.

Kobelev smiled. "Indeed. Three weeks ago our

people out there approached him with an offer of immediate cash help. He turned us down, of course. But over the next ten days his gambling losses took a sudden and very dramatic turn for the worse. We offered our help a second time."

"He turned you down again?"

"Flat," Kobelev said.

"You want me to go out there and convince him?" I asked.

"Yes, but not in the manner which you might expect."

I put my drink down on a low table between us. "You want Tripp fully converted."

"Exactly."

"And you have a plan in mind."

"Again correct. Tripp is married, has two children, a boy fifteen and a girl thirteen. I want you to kill one of them. We'll issue him a warning: Cooperate or we'll kill your other child and your wife."

Twelve

"I don't care which of Tripp's children you kill. I want it done quickly and cleanly, and then you are to get out of there."

Kobelev's words came back to me again as my watchdog Sergei Vladimirich Yerin and I climbed into a cab outside the terminal building at Istanbul's airport. He directed the driver to take us downtown to the Great Bazaar.

Early this morning my hair had been dyed a light blond, and I had been fitted with a matching mustache and contact lenses that made my eyes a pale blue, as well as a passport that identified me as Norbert Cartier, a South African diamond dealer.

All that had been accomplished at the dacha by ten A.M, and then a half an hour later Kobelev and Sergei had driven with me out to Frunze Central Airfield for the flight to Istanbul.

Kobelev had hinted the previous night, and again this morning, about a very large, very important mission that would be mounted within a week to ten days.

He had mentioned something about well-laid plans involving New York City. It explained the presence of Mikhail at the U.N. But Kobelev would not be more specific except to say that it would be the ultimate accomplishment of his career.

No further mention had been made of our duel the evening before, nor had Kobelev bothered to tell me anything about Yerin, except that he would accompany me and act as my backup in case something went wrong.

Tatiana had been very cool and distant during dinner, but her mother had been bright and vivacious during the long meal, asking me all about the latest fashions and fads for women in New York.

Everything had happened with such blinding speed, that until this moment I had had no real chance to think the entire situation out. Somehow I was going to have to take Yerin out, making it look like an accident, and then get word to Hawk, not only about this mission, but about the upcoming operation Kobelev had planned. If the New York thing was to be the madman's ultimate accomplishment, it would be awesome, and might be the very thing that would push the United States and Soviet Union into the war that Kobelev wanted.

Within twenty minutes the cabby had let us off in the middle of the Great Bazaar, which is the center of the city's shopping district. The huge area was filled with tens of thousands of people surging up and down the wide avenues lined with counters and stalls. Everything imaginable was for sale in this area; from meat and vegetables to fine linens; from copper and silver work to women and young girls.

Yerin had been close-mouthed during the two-and-a-half hour flight down from Moscow, answering the few questions I had asked him with little more than noncommittal grunts.

He was a short man, with a thin, sallow face and wispy white hair. He looked more like a bookkeeper than anything else, but from his manner, and the evident respect that Kobelev had shown him, I suspected he was a very efficient killer.

"Tripp never returns from his office before five in the afternoon," Yerin said as we strolled down one of the avenues. His English had an Oxford accent.

"What about his children?" I asked.

Yerin looked at me and grinned, the expression almost feral. "They return from school at precisely seven minutes after three which gives us around two hours. Plenty of time I should think."

"I don't think much of the idea of killing innocent children," I snapped.

Yerin's grin widened. "Except for the fact they generally present a smaller target, it's easy actually. You know they won't effectively fight back."

It took everything within my power not to kill the man on the spot. He was a child-killer, evidently an expert at it. I had heard of people like him, but before now I had never met one.

We turned down a narrow sidestreet four blocks from where the cab had dropped us off. Yerin seemed to know the way, and I assumed that we were rendezvousing with someone from

Moscow Station who would have an automobile and weapons for us.

The exchange, when it came, was very smoothly-managed. Had I not been watching for it, I would have missed the entire thing.

The little street was barely twenty-five feet wide, and crammed with people. About twenty feet ahead of us an old woman started shouting at one of the shopkeepers over the price of a vase, and while heads were turning that way, a tall man in workman's clothes elbowed his way between Yerin and me. At the moment he passed I caught the glint of a key in his left hand, which he slipped in Yerin's coat pocket and then was suddenly gone. A few seconds later we had passed the woman, and were soon out on one of the other main avenues.

Yerin hailed a cab, and when we were in the back seat he directed the driver to take us to the Admiralty Building, one of Istanbul's newer landmarks, a few blocks away.

"Nicely done," I said, half under my breath.

Yerin looked sharply at me, but said nothing until the cab dropped us off. After he paid the driver and we had started down the street, he said to me, sharply, "You talk too much."

"What's the matter, Sergei Vladimirich, are you frightened of me?"

He smiled, but said nothing as we continued around the block.

It was a few minutes past two thirty, and in half an hour Tripp's children would be returning from school. Our return flight to Moscow left at six o'clock, and once we made it out to the airport, and into the Aeroflot lounge, we would be supplied with diplomatic immunity, and no matter what the local authorities knew or suspected, we would not be detained.

A few blocks from the Admiralty Building, Yerin turned off the main street and entered a parking lot, where in one of the back rows he used the key to open the door of a small cream-colored Ford Cortina.

"Your weapon is beneath the seat," Yerin said to me once he was behind the wheel and had started the car.

As he backed out of the stall and headed for the parking lot exit, I reached beneath my seat and my fingers curled around the grip of a weapon which I pulled out. It was a 7.62mm Tokarev, a large silencer screwed on the end of the barrel. A very efficient weapon for medium-range work.

The clip was full, and before I laid the weapon out of sight beside me on the seat, I ejected a round into the firing chamber and checked to make sure the hammer was in the safety position.

Pera, the foreign quarter of Istanbul, is in the European side of the Bosporus, in the northern section of the sprawling metropolis. Yerin knew the city well. A few minutes before three he turned off the main channel highway into a neat and fairly well-maintained residential section where most of the European foreigners working in Istanbul had their homes.

Tripp's house was a moderately-sized brick structure with a central courtyard and a front gate. Yerin parked across the street about fifty feet up from the house and left the car idling.

He checked his watch. "Five minutes," he said, looking at me, a grin on his face. "They come by schoolbus which leaves them off at the corner. You can take one of them as they come down the street, and then we'll go immediately out to the airport."

I grabbed the gun and opened the car door. "I've got a better idea," I said getting out of the car.

"What are you doing?" Yerin shouted, lunging across the seat after me.

I stepped back out of his grasp. "Shut off the car and come with me," I snapped, looking across at the house. "Move it, we don't have much time!"

Yerin looked over his shoulder at the corner where the schoolbus would be coming in the next few minutes, then back out at me. "Get back here, Carter, before it's too late," he hissed.

"This is my operation, pal, and you're coming with me. Now move it!" I said. The gun was at my side, my thumb on the hammer, my finger on the trigger.

He looked at me for a long moment, hate and a bit of uncertainty in his eyes, but finally he turned back, shut off the engine, pocketed the key, and got out of the car.

"If you ruin this operation I will kill you," he said, as we went across the street.

"And if you interfere, Sergei Vladimirich, I will kill you," I replied. "So now that we understand each other, let's get on with it."

On the other side of the street, we approached

the front gate of Tripp's house. Yerin looked at his watch, and then glanced again toward the corner.

"His children will be arriving at any moment."

"I know," I said. "Ring the bell."

"What?" he sputtered.

"Ring the bell," I repeated. "We're going inside."

"Are you insane?"

"No, but I think you are. Either that or you're stupid. If we kill one of his children out here on the street, the other may come up with the registration number on our license plates. It's very possible that the Turkish police could stop us before we ever got close to the airport. Now ring the goddamned bell."

Yerin hesitated a moment longer, then reached out and yanked twice on the bell pull to the right of the thick wooden gate.

We could hear the bell tinkling somewhere inside the house, and a few moments later, as Yerin was reaching out to pull the cord again, the gate opened and Larry Tripp's wife was standing there.

"Yes?" she said. She was a small, plain-looking woman, dressed in slacks and a light-colored blouse. She seemed nervous.

"Mrs. Tripp?" I said politely. The gun was hidden at my side. "I'm Norbert Cartier, and this is my associate Mr. Yerin. We've come to talk to you about your husband."

An instant look of abject fear crossed her features. "Has something happened to Larry?"

"No," I said. "May we come inside. It will only take a moment.'"

She started to nod her head, but then something in Yerin's expression apparently spooked her, because her complexion went pale and she stepped back. "My God," she said. "You're Russians."

She tried to slam the heavy gate shut, but Yerin was too fast for her, and he started to shove his way inside. At that moment I stepped back and brought my left foot up and out and kicked him squarely in the back, sending him through the gate and tumbling to his hands and knees past the frightened woman.

Before the man could get back to his feet, I had stepped into the courtyard, slammed the gate shut behind me, and raised the pistol.

"Traitor," he shouted, and he started for me, but I raised the pistol a little higher, and shook my head.

Tripp's wife had turned and run into the house in the confusion, probably to call either the police or her husband. I hoped she had called Larry. If the Turkish police became involved in this, my mission would be finished.

Yerin was watching me through narrowed eyes. The slightest mistake on my part and he would spring for me. I would have to shoot him then, something I didn't really want to do unless I was forced into it.

If we could get in touch with Larry, and get him here, I could tell him what was happening, and Yerin could be put on ice long enough for me to return to Moscow, take care of Kobelev, and get out.

I started to move to the left, when Tripp's wife burst from the house, a .38 Smith & Wesson in her hands.

"Bastards," she shouted, and opened fire.

The first two shots were aimed at me, but they went wide as I leaped to the left. Yerin started toward her, at the same moment she had begun firing at him. The first two shots caught him in the chest, the third in his head, and the fourth crashed into the courtyard wall as he went down in a heap.

She had fired six times, and her pistol was now empty. I jumped up from where I had been crouched and raced to the woman, who turned the gun toward me and was wildly pulling the trigger, the hammer falling on empty barrels.

"It's all right now," I said reaching out for her.

She tried to hit me with the butt of the pistol, but I easily deflected the blow.

"Listen to me, Mrs. Tripp. The man you killed was sent here to murder one of your children."

"No," she screamed, backing up a pace.

"You must listen to me. I'm on your side," I said trying to reason with her. "Have you called your husband?"

She looked over my shoulder, her eyes suddenly widening. "Paul, Linda," she shouted. "Run! Get the police!"

I spun around on my heel in time to see the gate slamming shut. Her children must have come home. If they got the police now, everything would be ruined.

I started toward the gate when something very hard smashed into the back of my head, momentarily stunning me and causing me to stagger to my knees.

Somehow I managed to ward off a second blow as the woman swung the gun around toward my head, and I grabbed for her.

She was too quick for me, and in the next instant she had jumped back and raced into the house. I straightened up and took a step after her when I heard sirens in the distance.

There was no time now to deal with her, and there was even the possibility she was getting another weapon.

I hurried over to Yerin's body, where I grabbed the car key from his pocket, along with his identification and the airline tickets, then turned and went back through the gate and across the street where I leaped behind the wheel of the car.

The sirens were much closer by the time I had the Cortina started, and I quickly pulled away from the curb. As I turned the corner onto the main thoroughfare, three Turkish police cars were coming from the opposite direction.

I headed back into the city, careful to keep to the posted speed limit as I watched in the rearview mirror. The three police cars disappeared around the corner toward Tripp's house, and I sped up a little.

There was a possibility that Tripp's wife or one of the children had gotten a make and model on the car, which meant I was going to have to ditch it very soon. I'd take a cab immediately out to the airport, and duck into the Aeroflot lounge where I would be safe.

I glanced up in the rearview mirror again a few moments later in time to see one of the police cars careering around the corner, its blue light flashing as it came after me at high-speed.

"Damn," I swore, jamming the accelerator pedal to the floor. The little Ford shot ahead, but there was no way I would be able to outrun a police car with it.

At the next intersection I screeched around the corner, turned left a block later, and then turned into a narrow, twisting alleyway, locking the brakes fifty yards later.

Even before the car was fully stopped I had thrown open the door and jumped out, ducking in the back entrance of a building that turned out to be a restaurant. Before I hurried through, out to the front door, I stuffed the gun in my belt, and buttoned my coat.

Customers and waiters all looked up in surprise as I hurried through the restaurant, but no one said a thing to me, and within seconds I was out on the street.

Half a block away I flagged down a passing cab and jumped inside. The police had gotten to me too fast for a mere response to a call from an hysterical woman, which left only two possibilities that I could immediately think of. Either I had been spotted and identified at the airport, or Tripp's house was bugged. If the authorities suspected him of collusion with the Russians, they might have bugged his house and his phone. As soon as Yerin and I had shown up the alert would have been sounded. Either way, the airport was out.

"Take me to the Ürsküdar Ferry," I told the driver.

"Very good, sir," the man replied, and I sat way back in the seat as police cars began converging on the neighborhood we were leaving.

The first step would be for me to get away from the city, which would give me time to figure out my next move. There was another possibility that I would have to seriously consider, it occurred to me.

Kobolev's people had been trying to convert Larry Tripp for some time now, and it was very possible that the Soviets were also monitoring his house. If that were the case, they would have heard the exchange between Yerin and myself as well as between me and the woman. If I went back to the Soviet Union I would be a dead man.

It was a risk I was going to have to take, however. I had come too far, and had gotten too close to Kobelev to give it up now.

The cabby dropped me off at the ferry terminal on the Bosporous a few minutes later, just as the last of a string of automobiles and foot passengers were boarding one of the vessels.

I paid the driver and raced to the pedestrian turnstile where, for a few Turkish pounds, I purchased a ticket, and made it aboard just as the ramps were coming up. Within sixty seconds the boat was pulling out into the strait and I was on my way to Ürsküdar, one mile across on the Asian continent.

In reality, Istanbul, Fatih, Eyüp and Pera on the European side, and Ürsküdar on the Asian side, are all parts of one huge metropolis. But the flavor of the city across the Bosporus was immensely different from the one I had just left.

There was no doubt at all that Ürsküdar was Asian. The population was mostly Oriental, the slums more squalid, and the predominant mode of transportation off the main streets was a pedal-driven rickshaw.

From the ferry terminal I took a rickshaw to the train depot across town, where I went immediately to the telephone center inside and gave the clerk a number in the States.

It was nearly eleven at night on the east coast, so the international trunk lines were not very busy. Within a couple of minutes my call was going through and I was assigned a booth.

No one had followed me, I was reasonably sure of that. But if they had, my assignment would be ended anyway, so this call did not matter.

The phone was answered on the second ring by a very familiar voice. "Yes?"

"It's me," I said to Hawk.

"Where are you?"

"Ürsküdar."

"Are you in immediate trouble?" Hawk asked.

I glanced out of the phone booth across the busy terminal. No one seemed to be watching me, there was no one obviously loitering, and there were no policemen in sight. "No," I said. "But I may have some difficulty in getting back to Redland."

"Hold on a moment," Hawk said. I assumed he was putting a tape recorder on the line. A second later he was back. "Bring me up to date."

Quickly then, but using vague references to people and places in case the call was being monitored, I told Hawk everything that had happened to me from the moment I had taken Dr. Wells' car from the parking lot at the hospital until now.

He interrupted my story only twice: once to ask if I thought the story I had told them while I was being tortured was consistent with the story I had told them while I was drugged, and the second time to ask me if Kobelev's daughter could be an ally.

I could not answer either question, but of the two I was least certain about Tatiana.

When I was finished, Hawk was silent for a long while, the only sound on the line the static and hollowness of the international circuit.

"It's a very tricky situation, Nick. I cannot advise you. It must be your decision."

"I've already decided to return, sir," I said. "I'm going to need some help getting in. The airport in Stambul is out."

"What are the conditions for you there at the train depot?" Hawk asked.

"No unusual activity. But how long that will last is anyone's guess."

"All right," Hawk said. "Take the next train out to Ankara, and call me from there. In the meantime I'll get something set up for you."

"We're going to have to be very careful, sir," I said. "He's suspicious of me. When I come back without my watchdog, and without having accomplished this assignment it's going to be even worse."

"Not necessarily," Hawk said. "We may be able to use that to our advantage, especially in light of the fact that you say he has something very big planned for New York."

"Yes, sir."

"Call me from Ankara, Nick," he said. "And watch your step."

Thirteen

Although Ankara is less than two hundred fifty miles inland from Istanbul, the trip had taken nearly twelve hours by train, and I was bone weary by the time my call to the States went through and I was seated in a phone booth at the depot.

Hawk answered on the first ring. "Yes?"

"It's me," I said.

"Nick, get out of the depot immediately! The Turkish authorities are turning the country upside down for you, and the British have sent their big guns after you. Remember the part you were trained for. Now go!"

I slammed the phone down on its cradle, left the booth, and resisting the urge to run, headed at a steady pace toward the terminal doors to the street.

When I was about fifty feet from the exits, six uniformed Turkish policemen and two other men in civilian clothes barged through the doors.

I quickly stepped over to a newstand and buried my nose in a magazine as the eight men raced past me, across the terminal and down the stairs to the trains.

When they were gone, I glanced over toward the

doors where I could see at least two uniformed officers standing just outside.

They were after me, there was no doubt of it. And in just a minute or two the group that had gone down to the trains would realize that I had already arrived, and was probably somewhere within the depot. The call would go out then—for a tall blond man with pale blue eyes and a mustache.

I put the magazine down and hurried across the depot to one of the public restrooms, where I bought a towel from one of the attendants and went to a washbasin at the far end of the huge, crowded room.

No one paid the slightest attention to me as I ripped off the mustache, removed the contact lenses from my eyes, and quickly washed the water soluble blond dye out of my hair.

All that took less than five minutes, and when I was finished I went into one of the toilet stalls, where I took the gun from my belt, then took off my coat and draped it over my arm and hand so that the gun was not visible.

Back out in the terminal I stopped, and with one hand took out a cigarette and lit it as I let my gaze wander.

Several of the uniformed officers were standing by the stairs that led down to the trains. More uniformed policemen were posted at the terminal exits, and I spotted the two men in civilian clothes talking with the ticket agents.

People streamed in and out of the terminal, but the policemen did nothing more than closely scrutinize everyone who passed.

I headed across the terminal, my pace easy, as if

I were nothing more than a tourist come to see the Turkish capital.

As I approached one of the doors, the two cops there stiffened slightly and looked closely at me.

I smiled. *"Bon jour, Monsieur,"* I said to one of them.

The two cops looked at each other and shook their heads. When I'd gotten outside I quickly crossed the wide sidewalk and climbed into the back seat of a cab.

"The American Express office downtown," I said.

"Yes, sir," the cabby said, and he pulled away from the curb and headed toward town at breakneck speed.

I had been to Ankara only once, several years ago, and the only thing I really remembered about the city was that it was much cleaner and more modern than Istanbul. I also vaguely remembered that the Soviet Embassy was somewhere just off the downtown area.

Hawk had told me to play the part I had been trained for, which meant I would have to act like a Soviet agent in trouble in a foreign country. The most logical place for me to run to would be the embassy.

But the Turks and the British would have figured that as well, and would be waiting for me there. I would not be able to get within a hundred yards of the embassy gates. Not on my own.

Careful to keep the gun out of the cabby's sight in the rearview mirror, I stuffed it in my belt and then pulled my coat back on, buttoned it up and straightened my tie.

If I could get in the Soviet Embassy, a message

could be sent to Kobelev, and we could figure out some way of getting me back to Moscow. The only problem was one of time. In a very few days the Presidium would be meeting to consider his promotion.

It was noon by the time the cabby dropped me off in the heart of Ankara's modern downtown area, just across the broad avenue from the American Express office. I paid him, and when he had disappeared in the heavy traffic, I hurried down the block and around the corner, finding the post office and telephone center almost immediately.

I stepped up to the counter, where a clerk handed me the downtown directory, and I looked up the Soviet Embassy's number. In a local call booth, I dialed the number. It was answered on the first ring by a man speaking English.

"Good afternoon. This is the Embassy of the Union of Soviet Socialist Republics government. How may we be of service to you?"

"*Connect me with the director of the* Referentura," I snapped in Russian. That was the most secret section of any Soviet Embassy, in which local KGB operations were handled.

There was a dead silence on the line.

"This is Nick Carter. I'm in trouble. Now connect me with the director," I said urgently.

The connection was broken momentarily, a high-pitched whine came on the line, and then a man speaking in a low guarded voice came on over the top of it. "Where are you?"

"In the city. The Turkish police and British Secret Service are after me. They know I'm here."

"Where is Yerin?"

"Dead," I said.

"Can you find the mausoleum of Kemal Ataturk?"

"Yes."

"You will be picked up there within the hour." The high-pitched whine increased momentarily in volume, and then the connection was broken.

I hung up the phone and paid for my call at the counter, then left the post office and headed left, in the general direction of the mausoleum, one of Ankara's most notable buildings.

It was a sunny day, but very cold. Although there was no snow on the ground yet, it would come soon.

A few blocks from the post office I stopped at a large, crowded restaurant where I took a small table near the back. I ordered a glass of dark Turkish beer and a small plate of figs.

Hawk knew at least that something would be happening in New York, so that no matter how successful I was back in Moscow with Kobelev, his plans would be stopped. If nothing else, I thought, I had least accomplished that much.

When my order came, I paid the dark-skinned waiter, and slowly ate and drank. The mausoleum was less than three blocks away, if memory served me correctly, and I did not want to get there too early. Every second I was out on the street increased my chances of being spotted and arrested. I did not want to risk a shootout with the Turkish authorities or with the British Secret Service people. On the other hand, however, I hoped that Hawk hadn't tipped the British off that I was in reality not a traitor. That information would find its way to Kobelev very quickly, and my chances, which were slim enough already, would be reduced to zero.

I was finished with my light lunch a few minutes before one. I left the restaurant and headed quickly to the huge, ornately constructed building that housed the remains of Turkey's most significant patriot, Mustafa Kemal . . . better known by the people as Kemal Atatürk. It was Atatürk and his forces who had finally overthrown the oppressive rule of the sultan, and whose rallying cry had been: "Turkey for the Turks." Since that time, the Turks had looked at all foreigners through jaundiced eyes, and had developed a fearsomely nationalistic pride.

A half-block before the mausoleum, as I was about to cross the street, a black Citröen DS19 sedan pulled up to the curb, and the driver, a large, swarthy man, stuck his head out the window.

"Carter," he said. "Be quick." He spoke in English.

I backed up a pace, and my right hand went instinctively for the gun in my belt.

"I'm a friend," the man hissed. He looked both ways along the sidewalk. "Comrade Kobelev sent me," he said in Russian.

I hurried across the sidewalk as he opened the car door, and jumped in on the passenger side. Even before I had closed the door, he was pulling away from the curb, obviously very worried.

"I picked up a tail from the embassy, but I managed to lose them for a couple of blocks so that I could double back to pick you up," he said.

"Can you get me back to the embassy—" I

started to ask when he grabbed me by the collar and pushed me down to the floor.

"Get down!" he shouted. "They've picked us up again."

I crouched down on the floor of the car and pulled out my gun. The driver glanced down at me, and then up again at the road.

"Put that thing away," he snapped.

"I'm not going to be taken," I said looking up at him. Play the part, Hawk had said.

"You're jeopardizing our entire mission here."

"Tell that to Comrade Kobelev," I said. "If it hadn't been for Tripp's wife we would have been all right."

"I don't want to know," the driver said. "My orders are to get you up to Rize and nothing more."

"What's at Rize?" I asked.

"A boat, I think," he said. "Probably will take you across to Batumi."

We turned a corner and he sped up, turned another corner a few seconds later, and a third moments after that, finally swerving sharply to the right and slamming on the brakes as we entered a building. As I got up from the floor, a garage door was closing behind us, and the car door on my side was jerked open.

"Move it," someone shouted in Russian.

I leaped out of the car, and two men hustled me across the garage and bundled me into the back of a large, canvas-covered truck filled with live chickens in wooden cages.

As soon as I was inside the men stacked several other cages of chickens in the back of the truck, blocking the opening through which I had crawled, and then the tailgate was slammed shut and the canvas flap closed.

I just managed to sit down and brace myself against the stack of cages when the truck started, backed up, and then moved forward with a lurch. Heading toward Rize, which, if I remembered my geography correctly, is a small Turkish port on the Black Sea not too far from the Soviet border. But it had to be three hundred miles or more away, over at least one range of mountains.

It was going to be a long, hard trip that would take a dozen or more hours. Precious hours that were rapidly running out for my mission.

It had taken the better part of an hour of stop-and-go driving before we had finally cleared Ankara, and then the truck settled into a steady pace along what felt to me like a fairly well-maintained highway.

Several times we slowed down to barely a crawl, presumably as we passed through towns, but always within a few minutes the truck sped up again. This continued through the afternoon.

The chickens kept up a constant racket, and the stench in the back of the truck was nearly overpowering.

For a time, however, I actually managed to nod off, until in the early evening the temperature began to rapidly drop with the sun. I figured we must have been climbing into the mountains by now, although the Pontic Mountains, a very large chain, was near the Black Sea itself. How well the old truck would be able to manage some of those peaks was something that remained to be seen, but for now we had not been stopped, and were apparently making good time.

Around eight o'clock the truck slowed down again—for what I'd presumed was another town—but then pulled off to the side of the road and stopped.

I had been dozing, but instantly awoke, the gun in my hand, the safety off and my finger on the trigger.

The truck doors opened and then slammed shut, and I could hear someone talking but could not quite make out the words. A few moments later the canvas flap was pulled back, the tailgate clattered open, and someone was pulling the chicken crates aside.

I raised the gun.

Someone around the side of the truck said something about being careful, and whoever was moving the chicken crates stopped what he was doing. The man who had spoken laughed.

"Carter," a voice said in Russian, *"it is all right. You get off here."*

I held my silence.

"Carter," the man shouted a little louder.

Still I held my silence, training the gun toward the last few crates. After a moment the crates were pulled aside, and a man jumped up on the tailgate, started toward me, but then stopped when he saw that I was holding the gun on him.

"It's all right," he sputtered, slowly raising his hands above his head.

"Where are we?" I asked softly.

"Near Tokat. It's about halfway to Rize. Everything is all right. We have fresh clothes, food, and a car and driver for you. We haven't been followed."

"All right," I said finally. I eased the hammer back to the safety position, shoved the gun back in my belt and climbed out from behind the chicken crates as the man jumped down from the tailgate.

It was a moonlit night and crisply cold, but the air smelled sweet and fresh to me as I jumped down to the roadway and unlimbered my stiff legs.

The truck was parked on the gravel alongside a fairly wide, well-paved highway that wound its way east through a series of low foothills and snow-capped mountains.

A beat-up, old gray Mercedes four-door sedan was parked a few yards up the road from the truck, and in the illumination from the moon I could see a man seated behind the wheel, looking back at us.

"The chickens are going down to Tokat. Alexi will take you the rest of the way to Rize," the man who had come for me said. Another man stood beside the truck urinating into the ditch. He looked up at me and grinned.

"You smell like the chickens, Carter," he said laughing.

I had to laugh too. "And I feel like something they left at the bottom of their cages."

Both men laughed uproariously at my little joke, and the one who had opened the tailgate for me nodded toward the car. "Alexi is waiting, and he is a man of little patience," he said. "You must be at the boat before sunrise, and there is a long, hard way for you to go yet this night." He stuck out his hand and I shook it. "Good luck," he said.

"Yes," I replied, and then hurried up the road to the car.

The driver they called Alexi had gotten out from behind the wheel, and as I approached the car he opened the back door and pulled out a pair of slacks, a sweater, and a fur-lined jacket for me.

"Change out here," he said. "We'll put your old things in the trunk."

I quickly did as he said, and when we had stuffed my filthy clothing beneath the spare tire and other junk in the trunk, we climbed into the car. Alexi started it and then took off down the highway toward the distant mountains.

"There is food and a few beers in the back seat for you," he said. "In the glove box there are new identification papers for you in case we should be stopped."

"Do the authorities in Ankara know that I got out of the city?" I asked. I turned in the seat and grabbed the package of sandwiches from the back, along with a bottle of beer that was sealed with a rubber ring and porcelain cap held in place by a wire clip.

The driver glanced at me, disdain in his eyes. "Vladimir—the man from the embassy—was arrested by the Turkish police this afternoon. He is at the Cebeci Ordinance Army Barracks. He will talk soon, if he hasn't already."

"He knows that I'm on my way to Rize," I said.

The driver grunted, which I took to mean yes. It would not take the Turks very long to pry the information from the Russian, unless he was a very extraordinary man.

I found that I felt sorry for him, despite the fact

he was a KGB agent. The man had merely been
doing his job, helping a supposedly friendly agent,
and he would lose his life for his effort.

"Is there any way of helping him?" I asked.
"Any way of getting him out of there?"

"It is not your concern," the driver snapped.
"Now hold your silence. I do not wish to talk."

"That's fine with me, comrade," I snapped back,
and I turned my attention to the food and drink.

The transfer from the truck to the car had taken
place shortly after eight P.M., and for a solid six
hours we continued to climb in elevation, coming into the snow belt almost immediately and
rising above the tree line shortly before midnight.

The moon at this elevation, which had to be at
least twelve thousand feet above sea level, was
almost as bright as day. The road was moderately well maintained, although in a couple of
the high mountain passes, the car wheezing and
barely chugging along at less than half its power,
we had to force our way through small snow
drifts. In another few weeks, I suspected that
most of these roads would be closed until spring.

Shortly after two we came to the last high
pass, rounding a tight curve and topping a slight
rise—nothing now higher than the road we were
on. Then suddenly the Black Sea was below us,
sparkling like diamonds on a black velvet cloth
in the moonlight.

It was at least twenty-five miles away, and
more than twelve thousand feet below us, but it
looked as if we could reach out and touch it.
Rize itself, and another smaller town a few miles

up the shoreline to the east, stood out like yellow pincushions in the backdrop, and far out to sea, to the northwest, I could make out the lights of a freighter.

It was a stunning, beautiful sight that we didn't lose for at least two miles, until we reentered the tree line and the road began circling back and forth on itself as it unwound down to the sea.

Although the line-of-sight distance from the highest pass down to Rize was probably not much more than twenty-five miles, by winding road it was easily twice that far, and it was not until well after three thirty A.M. that we came into the seaport town.

Alexi skirted the main downtown section of the city, coming twenty minutes later to the waterfront area where hundreds of boats, most of them herring vessels, were tied up.

It seemed much colder down here than it had up in the mountains, due in part to the humidity here by the sea, but in a larger part due to my exhaustion and apprehension at returning to the Soviet Union.

If the Russians had bugged Tripp's house, and had monitored my conversation with Larry's wife, I would be a dead man the moment I stepped across the border.

Yet, I told myself, I had come this far, I was simply not going to give it all up now.

Alexi parked the car alongside a storage shed that lay across a wharf from a fishing vessel with the name *Tibili* painted across its bow in faded white letters. There were no lights on the boat, nor were any of the crew in sight.

"The *Tibili* is your boat," Alexi said. "They are waiting for you aboard."

"Where are you going?" I asked.

Alexi seemed to study my face for a moment. "Back to Ankara to see if I can't straighten out the mess you have caused us."

"Good luck," I said, and I climbed out of the car and went across the dock.

Even before I got to the boat, Alexi had pulled away from the shed, turned around, and then was gone, leaving me alone.

I jumped down onto the deck of the small ship and went around to one of the hatches. As I opened it and went inside, the engines started and I heard the scurrying of several men on the forward deck.

A couple of seconds later we were moving backwards from the dock, toward whatever awaited me back in the Soviet Union.

Fourteen

The Black Sea crossing to Batumi in Georgian S.S.R. posed no problems, although it took nearly eight hours. We were not pursued or challenged by any of the many Turkish patrol vessels in the area, and by noon I was aboard a military helicopter that took me up to a Soviet air force base near Krasnodar, two hundred seventy five miles to the northwest.

At two thirty in the afternoon I was hustled aboard a huge Tupolev cargo jet heading north, and a few minutes before four thirty, Moscow time, we were touching down at Frunze Central Airfield.

It had snowed quite heavily since I had left, and the weather had turned bitterly cold, a sharp wind taking my breath away as I hurried from the aircraft across the tarmac to a waiting car and driver.

I climbed in the back seat of the car, and the driver took off immediately across the field without a word.

Once we had cleared the airport and were headed toward the main highway, I sat forward in my seat.

"Where are you taking me?" I asked.

The driver glanced up at me in the rearview mirror. "To Comrade Kobelev's dacha, sir," he said crisply.

I sat back, smiling. If my treatment so far was any indication of what was to come, it was very likely that the Russians did not know what had actually happened in Istanbul.

But, and it was a very large but, I had no idea what Kobelev did know. I still had Yerin's identification papers and the other things I had taken from his pockets, and unless Kobelev gave me some kind of a clue, my story would have to be that Tripp's wife had a weapon, and had shot and killed Yerin before we had a chance to do anything about his children. She had disappeared after that, and I had time enough only to remove everything from Yerin's body that would identify him as a Russian and then get out of there.

"Is Comrade Kobelev at the dacha this afternoon?" I asked.

"No, sir," the driver said. "He asked me to convey his congratulations for a mission well done, and also asked me to convey his apologies for not being able to be with you for dinner this evening. He will be detained in the city until sometime tomorrow."

Congratulations. What the hell did that mean? Unless Hawk had been able to arrange something, some kind of a cover story for me and for Yerin's death. But what was it?

I was going to have to play this very carefully until I knew exactly what it was that I had supposedly accomplished in Istanbul.

But no matter what, I thought, tomorrow I would have to do what I had been sent here to do.

Tomorrow Kobelev would die, and I would have to somehow make my escape. It gave me a scant twenty-four hours or so to come up with some kind of workable plan.

It took nearly forty-five minutes for the drive out to Kobelev's dacha. Although the highway and then the driveway up to his place had been plowed recently, the wind had blown snowdrifts across the road every hundred yards or so. When we finally pulled up to the front door, the driver turned in his seat to me and smiled. "I must return to the city now, sir, but you may go directly in. They are expecting you."

"Thanks," I said. Exhausted, I got out of the car, mounted the steps onto the porch, and entered the house. To the right, soft music was playing in the main living room, and I headed past the stairs through the arch and into the huge room.

A fire was burning in the fireplace, and Kobelev's wife and daughter and the young army doctor were seated together, drinks in hand.

When I entered the room they all looked up. Katrina Fedorova seemed slightly bemused, and Tatiana seemed somewhat disappointed, but the doctor got to his feet and came unsteadily across the room to me, a wry smile on his lips.

"The favored son returns," he said, raising his glass in salute.

"Good afternoon," I said. "Will you offer me a drink, or am I to go thirsty?"

"By all means," the doctor said, bowing slightly. He was drunk. "Let me attend."

He started to turn away, but I reached out and grabbed his arm. "What's the problem, Doctor?" I asked, my voice low enough so that Tatiana and her mother could not hear me.

The doctor looked into my eyes, disgust on his face. "I have a certain amount of trouble dealing with your type."

"What the hell do you mean by that?"

The man seemed suddenly unsure of himself; as if he had stepped over some invisible boundary but now it was too late for him to back away. "I mean simply that I find war terrible enough, but when a child is murdered I have trouble dealing with it."

So that was it. Hawk had done his work well. Tripp and his wife had to be super actors. But it gave me a strange feeling now, looking into the doctor's eyes. Technically he was the enemy, and yet he was a good man.

"There are many things you cannot possibly understand, Doctor," I said. "Heal the sick, and leave it at that."

"What are you two talking about over there?" Katrina Fedorova said, getting to her feet.

The doctor looked over his shoulder at her. "Pardon me, Madam Kobelev, but I don't feel well. Please excuse me," he said. He looked back at me, and then left the room.

"Come in, Nicholas," Kobelev's wife said. "Have a drink before dinner with us."

Suddenly I felt dirty. I had come to kill this woman's husband. I couldn't bring myself to sit with her and talk about the weather.

"I'm sorry," I said. "I'm not feeling very well myself, and I think I should go up to my room. Would it be possible to have my dinner sent up?"

"Of course . . ." the woman was saying as I turned on my heel and went upstairs to my room.

I still had the weapon that I had gotten in Istanbul, and already the glimmering of an idea was beginning to form in my mind—a workable idea, even though at this moment it was distasteful to me.

Tomorrow I would convince Kobelev that he and I should go into Moscow. To Lubyanka. Alone. On the way I would kill him, and then immediately go to the embassy.

From that point on it would be a matter for the politicians, but the major threat—Kobelev—would be gone.

I took off my jacket and threw it over a chair, then stuffed the gun under my pillow on the bed. I went into the bathroom and began running water in the tub. When I returned to the bedroom a moment later, Kobelev's wife was leaning against the door, a little smile on her lips and a brandy snifter in each hand.

"You didn't stop for a drink, so I thought I'd bring one up to you," she said softly.

She was dressed in a pair of slacks and a thick sweater.

"Should you be here?" I asked, stopping just within the room.

"Delicious," she said laughing. "Or as Niki would say, 'rich.' "

I didn't move, nor did I say a thing. Going to bed with a man's daughter, if discovered, gave me at least the elements of a reasonable defense. But making love with the man's wife was impossible.

She pushed away from the door, then came across the room to me swaying a bit, and I suspected she was a little drunk. She handed me my drink.

"Poor Nicholas," she said looking into my eyes.

"You think murdering an innocent child is difficult, wait until you have to return home and assassinate your own president."

I had brought the glass up to my lips, but my throat constricted and I couldn't drink. "What?" I said.

She smiled wanly and nodded her head. "You're his star pupil, didn't you know? He means to bring us all to war. You're to assassinate your own president, and then he will expose you. Delicious."

"Why are you telling me this?" I asked.

The smile left her lips. "Stop him, Nicholas. The Soviet Union doesn't want war with the United States."

"Why doesn't your own Presidium stop him?"

She waved it off. "The old fools are all frightened of him. Don't you know that? No one in this country can stand up to him."

"So what is it you want me to do, Katrina Fedorova, murder your husband?"

"Yes," she said, her voice suddenly sharp. She turned away, not able to face me for the moment. "He sees himself as a despot. Organized society will end with the nuclear war between our countries, and Niki will become the Mongul king of the European Russias."

I laughed, and she spun around to me.

"Don't take it so lightly, my American friend. What I have told you is true. Niki means to become ruler of a kingdom. A Russian Camelot."

"Is he insane?" I asked.

She shook her head. "Not as you mean the word, no. But he is not of this time. He should have lived five hundred years ago."

"He doesn't have the authority to order the assassination of my president," I said.

"Not at the moment. But within two days he will. The Presidium will elect him Operations Chief for the *Komitet*. Then he will be able to do anything he wants."

"If, as you say, everyone knows that his aim is to embroil us in nuclear war, then they won't elect him."

"Oh, yes they will, my naive Nicholas, oh, yes they will. They are all frightened to death of him, believe me. They feel compelled to do his bidding."

"Incredible," I said.

"No more incredible than your real purpose here."

I arched my right eyebrow—but said nothing.

"You should have guessed by now Nicholas that almost everyone knows why you are here."

"Indeed," I said.

"Indeed," she snapped. "At Lubyanka at this moment are the troops who will be assigned to Niki once he is promoted. When that happens he will be an untouchable. Everyone knows Niki is to be elected chief. Ask yourself why those troops haven't already been assigned out here."

"Your husband has not yet been elected."

"Don't be a complete fool. Even in your own country when one of your candidates wins a few primary elections you provide Secret Service bodyguards. Months ago Niki should have been assigned a contingent. But it hasn't happened because everyone is hoping he will be assassinated."

"Why haven't I been executed then?" I said.

Katrina laughed, the sound of it almost musical. "My dear Nicholas, you flatter my husband. Your presence here has inflated his sense of self-importance higher than it has ever been. I honestly think he was disappointed when you didn't kill him during your duel.''

I turned and went across the room to the dresser, above which was hanging a painting of a Russian Orthodox Church. I reached up and gently moved the painting away from the wall, but there was nothing behind it except for the wallpaper. Next I checked the table lamp beside my bed and the drapes on the windows, still with no results. Finally I set my drink down and went to the bed, where I got down on my hands and knees and looked under it at the springs. The microphone was attached with a small wire clip near the headboard.

Kobelev had known all along that I had made love with his daughter, and now he knew everything that his wife and I had said to each other. I yanked the tiny pickup from where it was attached, then got to my feet and tossed it across the room to her.

She caught it with fumbling hands, and when she realized what it was, she dropped her glass, her complexion turning a pasty white.

"I . . . " she said; but then she turned, pulled open the door, and was gone.

I had suspected my room was bugged, but until now it hadn't made much difference. I just wondered how Kobelev was going to take his wife's blatant disloyalty. Perhaps it didn't matter to him. Perhaps that's why he kept his wife and daughter out here at the dacha practically as prisoners.

At the door I looked out into the deserted corridor. The music was still playing downstairs in the living room, but other than that the house was quiet.

After a moment I closed the door and then cleaned up the mess from where Katrina had dropped her drink. Then I stripped off my clothes, grabbed the brandy she had brought me, and went into the bathroom where I lowered myself into the steaming hot tub, closed my eyes, and let my mind relax. I would need all the rest I could get, because tomorrow things were going to heat up around here.

The masseur came up half an hour later as I was drying myself off, and after a quick massage I dropped off to sleep on the table. At eight o'clock sharp one of the house staff brought my dinner to me along with a bottle of French cognac and more cigarettes.

Within twenty minutes I had finished the borscht, had eaten the tasty meat and vegetable stew, had one small drink, and then climbed gratefully between the sheets, falling instantly into a dreamless sleep.

I awoke sometime around four in the morning, and for a while I just lay in bed listening to the house creaking from the below-zero weather. Finally, however, I got out of bed, lit myself a cigarette and went to the window and looked out. The bright moon illuminating the snow-covered forest made it all seem like something out of a fairy tale.

My conscience was beginning to bother me. Despite what Kobelev had done, what the man was, and what he would probably do if left to his own devices, I was still having trouble dealing with killing him in cold blood.

It wasn't a matter of me backing out of this assignment. I would kill the man at the appointed hour. But I didn't like it.

Perhaps I should have killed him during our duel when I had the chance. If what Katrina Fedorova had told me was true, probably nothing would have happened to me, except that I would have been given every opportunity to escape the country.

A small deer emerged from the woods at the back of the house, stopped for a moment in the clearing, and then bounded off.

The Soviet Union was a beautiful country, its people for the most part no different than anyone else in the world. But for men like Kobelev, and even worse, men who allowed his kind to flourish, Russia could be among our closest friends.

I turned, suddenly cold, and went across the room to my closet where fresh clothes were hanging. I pulled on a pair of trousers, a light pullover sweater and my shoes, and then left the bedroom and went downstairs.

A fire was still burning in the living room fireplace, and after I had poured myself a cognac, I went over to it, and, leaning forward and resting one hand on the high mantel, I stared into the flames. Despite its warmth, I was still cold. I wanted this assignment to be over with right now.

I heard a rustling of fabric behind me, and turned as Katrina Fedorova, dressed in a thick robe and slippers, her hair pinned up at the back, came across the room to me.

"I couldn't sleep either," she said.

When she reached me she took the drink from my hand and sipped it, then handed it back.

"Do   you   always   begin   your   day   like

this . . . with a drink?" she asked.

"Hardly ever," I said. I set the glass on the mantel and she came, shivering, into my arms.

"My dear sweet American," she said. She smelled fresh of lilac soap and a faint perfume. "I think I signed our death warrants by my stupid comments last night."

"Can you get to the recording equipment and erase the tapes?" I asked, speaking softly into her ear.

"No," she said. "I tried. But as far as I can tell the wires run downstairs to the telephone terminals. Probably connected to his office in the city." She looked up into my eyes. "So you see, it doesn't matter any longer if you are really a defector, or if you've come here to kill him."

"It doesn't matter to whom?" I asked.

She smiled sadly. "I want you to make love to me, Nicholas."

Her head went back a little farther, her eyes closed, and I drew her to me and kissed her deeply, her lips full and sensuous, her body mature but still firm.

"Nicholas," she said when we parted. Her eyes were moist. "Please."

Without a word I led her across the living room and out into the entry corridor where we started slowly up the stairs. This was worse than foolish, it was insane. I knew it, and yet at the same time I desired her as much as she evidently wanted me, even though my conscience was really taking a battering now. I had made love with Kobelev's daughter, I was about to make love with his wife, and tomorrow I had to kill him.

Halfway up the stairs the front door banged

open and Kobelev strode into the entryway as Katrina and I turned and looked down.

He came to the foot of the stairs at the same moment his wife pulled away from my arm and took a step down toward him. He pulled a pistol from his jacket pocket, raised it and fired.

His wife was flung against the bannister, a bright red stain spreading across the front of her robe, and then she collapsed, pitching forward and tumbling down the stairs to his feet.

I was too far away to make a try for him, and I was totally exposed, bracketed for an easy shot by the stairwell.

"You heard then," I said.

"Everything," he replied calmly.

The pistol was at his side, and I took a step down, but he raised the gun. Where the hell was the house staff?

"In thirty-six hours I will become the director of the *Komitet*, and then no one will be able to stop me," he said.

"You mean to assassinate my president?" I asked.

"Yes," he said. "Mikhail was to do it when your president comes to New York in two weeks."

"You were going to use your own stepson?" I said. "And then expose him?"

"Of course," Kobelev said matter of factly. "Your arrival was most fitting. You would have replaced him quite nicely."

"And now?" I asked. I started to take another step down, but Kobelev raised the pistol so that it was pointing directly up at me, and I stopped, my left foot still in mid-air.

"And now I will have to find someone else for my little project."

"It won't work . . . " I started to say, when Tatiana rushed from her father's study."

"Papa," she shouted as she raced across the corridor toward him.

Kobelev half turned as Tatiana reached him, her right hand coming up, something glinting in the dim light, and then plunging toward her father.

Kobelev grunted, fired his pistol, the shot going far wide of me, then staggered backwards. "Peatrina," he said, the pistol slipping out of his hand.

"Bastard," Tatiana hissed.

And then Kobelev crumpled to the floor on his back, the handle of a letter opener protruding from his chest.

Fifteen

Tatiana stepped back away from her father's body at the same moment a car door slammed and someone came up on the porch.

I raced down the stairs and at Kobelev's side snatched the pistol from his slack grasp, and raised it as the front door slammed open and Kobelev's driver burst into the entryway, an automatic in his hand.

I fired at the same moment he started to raise his gun, and he was flung backwards, crashing against the door and shattering the frosted glass pane.

"Bastard!" Tatiana screamed hysterically down at her father's body.

The letter opener had apparently penetrated his heart, killing him instantly. There was no blood.

The young army doctor appeared at the head of the stairs as I got to my feet and turned to look up. He was holding a gun in my general direction.

"Go back to your room, Doctor," I called up to him.

Tatiana was crying now, unable to take her eyes off the bodies of her father and mother.

"Did you kill that child in Istanbul?" the doctor asked, his voice slurred from alcohol.

"No," I said. Every muscle in my body was tense. The pistol I was holding loosely at my side was ready to fire, the hammer back, a live round in the chamber. In a split instant I could feint to the right, bring the gun up and kill the doctor. But I didn't want to do that. He was a good man. There had been enough senseless killing in this assignment without adding another death.

"I believe you," the doctor said lowering his pistol. He turned and without a further word disappeared down the corridor.

I turned and bolted for the door, jumping over Kobelev's body, but Tatiana leaped toward me and grabbed me by the arm.

"No," she screeched. "Don't leave me here!"

I hesitated for only a moment. If I left her she would become the scapegoat. Someone was going to have to pay for Kobelev's murder. She would be the one.

"All right," I snapped, pulling out of her grasp. "Are there guards outside?"

"No . . ." she started to say, but then changed her mind. "I don't know. There might be."

"Stay behind me," I said. "But keep down." I stepped over the body of Kobelev's driver, my shoes crunching on the broken glass, then bent down and retrieved his automatic.

I opened the front door just a crack and looked outside. It was bitterly cold, but except for the black Zil limousine parked in the driveway, there was nothing else in sight.

"Come on," I said over my shoulder. I shoved the front door all the way open, raced across the porch, down the steps, and around the hood of the car to the driver's side.

Tatiana was climbing in the passenger side as I slipped behind the wheel. The engine was running, but the headlights had been switched off. I flipped them on.

When Tatiana had her door closed, I slammed the big car in gear and took off down the driveway toward the highway. It would not be very long before the alarm was raised, if it hadn't been already, but I was hoping that in the confusion I would be able to make it to the American Embassy in downtown Moscow. It was a very slim chance. But we had no other at the moment.

The wind had died down and the road had been cleared of drifts, but it was still slippery. When we hit the end of the driveway and came around the corner onto the highway, the big car spun around, almost going into the ditch.

Tatiana was white-faced, and she had braced herself against the door, one foot up on the dashboard.

"Where are we going?" she shouted.

"Into the city," I said once I had the car under control and we were racing down the highway.

"To your embassy?" she screamed. "We'll never get to it. They have it guarded twenty-four hours a day."

There was no one behind us yet on the highway. I reached down and grabbed the radiotelephone from its cradle below the dash, but before I hit the push-to-talk switch, I glanced at Tatiana. She was staring wide-eyed at me.

"Is this connected with the city telephone system, or does it connect with Lubyanka?" I asked.

She was shaking her head. "I don't know," she said. "I don't know."

I hit the push-to-talk switch, and an instant later a man was on the line.

"Central Control."

"Traffic from Comrade Kobelev," I snapped gruffly in Russian.

"Yes, sir," the operator said crisply.

"I want a clear connection with the American Embassy," I said.

"Sir?" the operator said confused.

"You heard me!" I shouted.

The phone went dead, and after several seconds I was about to put it down when there was a soft burring, and a young woman answered. "The United States Embassy, may I help you?"

"Marionette," I shouted. "This is Nick Carter. Marionette."

"One moment, sir," the woman said, her voice maddeningly calm.

A second or two later a man was on the line. "Carter, where are you?"

"Hollinger?" I shouted into the phone.

"This is Hollinger. Where are you calling from?"

"The Circumferential Highway. I'm on my way in. . ." I was saying when the phone went dead.

At that same moment I glanced up into the rear-view mirror. There were at least three sets of head-lights behind me, gaining fast. I dropped the phone and jammed the accelerator pedal to the floor, the big car surging ahead.

Tatiana swiveled around in her seat and looked out the rear window. I had laid the guns down on the seat beside me, and a moment later she had turned back, grabbed the automatic and was cranking down the window on her side.

The car was instantly filled with an unbelievably cold wind. "What the hell are you doing?" I shouted.

"Just drive!" she snapped, and she stuck her arms and head out the window, raised the gun and began firing at the cars behind us.

I held the big limousine as steady as I could, and on the sixth shot the lead car behind us swerved to the left, then to the right, and finally burst into a bright ball of flame as it skidded sideways and began to roll.

Tatiana pulled back inside the car and rolled the window up. "That should hold them for a little while . . ." she started to say, but her voice died in mid-sentence.

To the right in the distance Frunze Central Airfield was lit up in the early morning darkness. Straight ahead down the highway, however, were at least a half dozen vehicles, their lights flashing. It was a roadblock.

I hit the brakes and the big car fishtailed to the right. Instantly I steered into the skid, but we hit another patch of glare ice and the back end of the car swung completely around. We were sliding totally out of control.

It all seemed to be happening in slow motion. I had time to grab the pistol from the seat behind me and then brace myself as the car dropped off the side of the road down into the ditch. We started to roll, but then flipped around backwards, snow flying everywhere.

We stopped suddenly, the engine killed, the headlights shining back up toward the highway fifty yards above, and the silence was deafening.

Tatiana had struck her head on the windshield and there was a thin trickle of blood from her nose. She was unconscious but she was breathing regularly.

In the distance I could hear sirens. The window on my side had shattered, and through the open space I could see the lights of the airport three quarters of a mile away across a snow-covered field. A large airliner was parked in front of the terminal building. It was our only out. I figured if we could get to the airliner, and hold it hostage it would give Brad Hollinger time to figure something out.

I opened my door, climbed out of the car and worked my way through the snow to the other side, where I yanked opened the passenger door.

Tatiana was starting to come around as I pulled her out of the car. At that same moment the first vehicles from the roadblock were pulling up on the highway above us.

I threw her over my shoulder and headed away from the car directly across the field toward the airport. But within twenty-five yards I knew it was useless. The snow was hip-deep in most spots, and neither of us was dressed for the bitter cold.

The field was totally bare of trees, and it was at least a half-mile through the snowdrifts to the end of the plowed runway.

A helicopter lifted off from near a hangar next to the terminal and within a few seconds it headed directly for us, a bright spotlight searching the field below it.

I lay Tatiana down on top of the snow and, steadying the pistol with both hands, took aim on the rapidly approaching machine. Before it came within range, however, a second and third helicopter lifted off and headed our way as well. From behind us I could also hear the sounds of several snowmobiles revving up.

For a couple of long seconds, as the first helicopter came within range, I had it in the sights of my pistol, but then I lowered the gun, threw it down in the snow, and picked up Tatiana.

The lead helicopter, equipped with big pontoons, set down a hundred feet away from us, while the other two machines hovered in position to the left and right.

Two men in army uniforms jumped out of the machine, and pushed their way through the snow to us, the wind from the rotors making it nearly impossible to see more than a few feet.

One of the men took Tatiana from me, and the other one helped me back to the helicopter. It seemed as if both men were nervous; the one helping me kept looking back toward the highway, where the sound of the snowmobiles was quite loud now.

As soon as we had piled into the chopper the pilot lifted off, swung around over the approaching snowmobiles that had come down from the highway, and headed back to an airliner parked in front of the terminal.

"What's going on?" I shouted over the noise of the screaming engine. "Where are you taking us?"

The man who had helped me was strapped in one of the front seats, and he turned around and leaned back toward me. "We're getting you out of the country," he shouted. He pointed down toward the airliner now less than a quarter of a mile away. "TWA," he shouted. "It's ready to leave. You're going to be on it."

"I don't understand," I shouted. "What about the girl?"

The man looked at Tatiana, whose eyes were fluttering. "She did the killing, didn't she."

I nodded.

"Take her with you," he snapped.

"Why . . . " I started to ask, but by then we had come in low over the big jet and were touching down. Immediately the man who had helped me unstrapped himself from his seat and kicked the door open.

"The girl," he shouted. "Hurry!"

I yanked Tatiana out of the seat and down to the pavement, where half a dozen soldiers immediately helped us across the parking ramp and up the boarding stairs into the airliner.

Once we were inside, the stairs were pulled away, and one stewardess hustled us down the aisle, while another was closing and dogging the hatch.

The aircraft was filled with passengers, some of them sleeping. Even before we got to our seats, the engines were started and the big plane began to roll.

We were out at the end of the runway by the time Tatiana and I were strapped in a pair of seats near the back, and the stewardess barely had time to strap herself down when we were accelerating toward takeoff.

"What's happening to us?" Tatiana suddenly screamed.

"It's all right now," I said, reaching over and grabbing her by the shoulders.

She looked at me, wide-eyed. "Where are we going? What has happened?"

"I don't know how, but we're aboard an American airliner."

The aircraft's landing gear was pulled up, the flaps retracted, and soon the big jet banked gently to the north as it continued its climb out over Moscow.

A few minutes after we had taken off, the stewardess who had closed the front hatch came down the aisle to me.

"The captain would like a word with you on the flight deck, Mr. Carter," she said softly.

I unbuckled my seat belt and got up. The other stewardess had gotten out of her seat as well. "I'll take care of the young lady," she said.

"Don't worry," I said to Tatiana in Russian. "Everything will work out."

Then I turned and went up the aisle, most of the passengers now awake and staring curiously up at me as I passed.

The stewardess knocked once on the flight deck door, then opened it and stepped aside. "Go right in, sir," she said to me.

"How about fixing me up with a very large whiskey on the rocks?" I asked.

The young woman smiled. "Right away, sir," she said.

I stepped past her onto the crowded flight deck and she closed the door behind me. All three officers looked up.

"Carter?" the man in the left seat said.

"Right," I replied.

"Bill Demming," he said. "We were wondering when you'd show up."

"How did you know I was coming?" I asked, confused. This wasn't making any sense.

"The Soviet Air Force liaison officer for Frunze Airfield told us you were being ejected from the country, and that we were to hold for you. Do you mind telling me what the hell you did?"

The navigation officer had gotten up from his seat and he offered it to me. "I'm going back for some coffee," he said. "Welcome aboard."

"Thanks," I said, shaking his hand. I slipped into his seat, and the copilot stuck his hand out.

"Stewart Granger," he said.

I shook his and then the captain's hand. "Where are we headed?"

The copilot grinned. "Over the Pole to New York direct. Finally."

"We were scheduled to take off at eleven last night," Captain Demming said. "So we've been aboard, ready to go, for seven hours. Now what in hell did you do?"

It all suddenly became clear to me. Katrina Fedorova had been at least partially correct, incredible as it was.

No one wanted a war with the United States, and there apparently was a faction that realized Kobelev was leading them toward one. I had been pegged as his assassin, and whoever was in control of the opposition had waited for me to do the job I had been sent to do.

They must have figured it was going to happen last night, reasoning that I would have to kill him before he was promoted. Once it was done they would hustle me out here to this plane and allow it to take off.

But that meant someone must have been watching Kobelev's dacha. Someone on the staff evidently was passing information.

It was incredible.

The captain was staring at me, waiting for my answer. What *had* I done to be kicked out of the country? Not a thing, I thought. Not a thing.

Epilogue

A light snow was falling from a slate gray sky as I climbed out of the back seat of a limousine parked on First Avenue in front of the United Nations building.

Roadblocks had been placed at every intersection up to Forty-eighth. A half a block south, at the corner of East Forty-second, four black and whites were parked, their lights flashing. And here at the U.N. Plaza itself were another five units. Secret Service agents mingled with the crowd of about five hundred people.

I walked back to a plain gray sedan with government tags as Saul Breitlow, the agent in charge of the New York FBI office, got out from the driver's side.

When I reached him we shook hands.

"Did she spot anyone?" he asked.

I shook my head. "I don't think they'll go through with it now."

Breitlow was a huge man, something over six-feet-five, with a frame to match. "I wish I could share your confidence," he said. He looked past me toward Forty-second Street.

"Have you got their people tagged?" I asked.

He looked back. "The worrisome ones. It'd be impossible to watch all two hundred of them. We'd be tripping over each other."

Suddenly, in the distance, we heard the faint sounds of sirens, and Breitlow stiffened. "Here he comes," he said. He turned on his heel and went back to his car, where he grabbed his walkie-talkie and began issuing instructions to his people stationed at a dozen key spots around the area.

I went back to my car and opened the door for Tatiana.

"Is he coming?" she asked slipping out.

"He'll be here in a minute or two," I said.

She let her gaze slowly roam through the crowd, the sirens coming much closer, and then she shook her head.

"Nothing?" I asked.

"No one I recognize, Nicholas."

The lead escort motorcycles and other vehicles in the presidential motorcade came around the corner on Forty-second, and raced up to a halt directly in front of where we were parked. A second or two later the president's limousine turned the corner, pulled up, and was immediately surrounded by a dozen Secret Service agents.

"Anything yet . . . " I started to ask, when Tatiana stifled a scream and pointed toward the crowd across the street.

"There!" she said.

I took a step away from her as I started to pull out my Luger. At that same moment President Robert Manning was climbing out of his limousine, and Tatiana pulled something from her purse and darted toward him.

"Get down!" I shouted as I started to bring my gun around.

Tatiana fired, hitting a Secret Service agent standing next to the president as two other agents knocked Manning to the pavement. Saul Breitlow came running around his car.

She fired a second shot that went wild and a split second later I fired, hitting her low in the back, and she fell to the pavement as the crowd finally began to react, people racing in every direction.

Hawk was staring out the window of his office down at the traffic on Dupont Circle as I finished the almost unbelievable case file report he had handed to me without comment half an hour ago.

I closed the cover and softly laid the bulky file on his desk, then sat back in my chair. Hawk turned around, looked down at me a moment, then sat down himself.

"We're sure about this?" I asked, finding it difficult to say much of anything.

"The window on her side was open. Someone from the crowd must have tossed her the weapon."

"I mean everything else, sir," I said.

"Dr. Wells could find no traces of subliminal conditioning in the girl. So what she told us under drugs has to be regarded as the truth."

"She didn't kill her father after all," I said. "It was all an act."

Hawk was nodding. "He murdered his wife and used his own daughter."

"How about his promotion? The Presidium was supposed to act on it?"

"We believe that was all a sham, too, although if

he had actually managed to assassinate the president he might have gotten it."

"He out-maneuvered us all," I said.

"And probably will try again," Hawk said. He lit himself a cigar.

"What about Tatiana?"

"She'll be all right. The bullet cracked a couple of ribs, did some kidney damage, but it missed the spinal cord. Hospitalization for a couple of months, then convalescence for a few more months."

"And after that?" I asked.

"I don't know, Nick. Maybe she'll end up being the key to her father after all. Maybe we'll have to beat him at his own game. He will have to be stopped."

There was nothing left to say now. After a while I got up and headed for the door.

"I want you back here Monday morning bright and early," Hawk said pulling another file folder from a stack on his desk.

"Yes, sir," I said without looking back. Right now, I was in need of a bath, some fresh clothes, and a very large bourbon. I'd worry about Monday when it came.

DON'T MISS THE NEXT NEW
NICK CARTER SPY THRILLER

NORWEGIAN TYPHOON

"You are an idiot, Gorman," she raged. "You are failing the cause."

"Cause be damned. This is a system designed not to be easily broken. How am I supposed to do it on command?"

"Because *I* order it!" Thierkelsen said haughtily.

They grumbled and yelled at the others gathered about, trying to affix blame wherever possible. I silently stole away, secure in the knowledge that the Russians had built a better control system than I'd given them credit for. This design paranoia on their part took some of the pressure off me. The missiles took care of themselves; their nuclear sword was sheathed. I could concentrate on the atomic reactor powering this entire beast.

Disable it and I'd disable the entire Typhoon submarine. I felt the lining of my jacket to make sure I still carried the transponder. It had been quite a few hours since I'd activated it—too many for my peace of mind. By now, Hawk should have had the entire Sixth Fleet out of the Mediterranean and breathing down the Lenin's periscope.

But I hadn't even heard any conversation about a possible hunt going on. I had to assume that help was still a long way off and that I was on my own.

I ran down the corridor leading to the reactor room. I burst inside breathless, and called to the woman working the panel, "Thierkelsen wants you. Now!"

"What? Again. Oh," she said, stamping her heavily booted foot in disgust. "Take over."

She was almost out the hatch when she realized mine was a new face, one she hadn't seen. Even with as many of the *Norge i Morgen* terrorists as were aboard the *Lenin*, they'd trained together and were at least vaguely familiar with one another.

"You . . . you're!" she started. I shoved her hard and sent her sprawling into the corridor I'd just vacated. Slamming the door, I dogged it down all around. Then, to make sure it'd stay, I smashed a desk chair from a nearby console and wedged the broken legs against the dogs. Eventually, they could knock down the door but it'd take time. And time was what I needed most right now.

She pounded fruitlessly on the door with her fists. Good. Let her waste valuable time. The longer she stayed trying to break in by herself, the longer it would be before Thierkelsen came with cutting torches or explosives to blow the door. While the hatches were designed for emergency use against leaks, the doors themselves were something of a joke in that respect. Any leak occurring at the depths the *Lenin* traveled at would be deadly. No single door protected as well as a foot-thick titanium hull. If the leak came at less than a hundred yards under the surface, those doors might be worth something.

I was satisfied that they were strong enough to keep out a small army for a short while.

I turned and looked over the controls the woman had just left. Green lights indicated the reactor functioned perfectly. It was my duty to throw a monkey wrench into its workings.

While the layout and design were different than what I'd trained on, the basics remained the same. I found the fast neutron counter and played with the dials until the count started up—this meant I'd started the cadmium control rods on their inexorable way out of the pile. Soon, the neutron radiation environment would be intolerable. The heat would mount, stainless steel piping would flow like butter in the summer sun and the plutonium rods themselves would start to puddle.

When melt-down occurred, that puddle of plutonium would go right through the bottom of the steel and concrete containment vessel and out into the ocean.

The fast neutron count mounted satisfactorily. The *Lenin* would die and take all those aboard with its death throes.

Though I've often been confronted with life-or-death situations, seldom has the option appeared where killing myself to succeed in my assignment became a consideration. There didn't seem any other way now. Sooner or later Thierkelsen and her crew would discover the way around the Soviet computer block and those birds would fly with their atomic warheads. This eliminated the missiles, warheads, and the torpedoes slated for North Sea drilling rigs.

It's not easy watching your own death unfold, especially when all you have to do to stop it is reach out and turn a single dial. But I watched. The fast neutron count mounted.

Sirens went off.

Red lights flashing all around, I knew I'd reached a danger point. Automatic alarms signaled any operator to get a move on and check the panel. I studied it to make sure the slow pulling of the control rods continued according to schedule . . .

—From NORWEGIAN TYPHOON
A new Nick Carter Spy Thriller From
Ace Charter in April

FROM THE NICK CARTER
KILLMASTER SERIES

☐ **TEMPLE OF FEAR**	80215-X	$1.75
☐ **THE NICHOVEV PLOT**	57435-1	$1.75
☐ **TIME CLOCK OF DEATH**	81025-X	$1.75
☐ **UNDER THE WALL**	84499-6	$1.75
☐ **THE PEMEX CHART**	65858-X	$1.95
☐ **SIGN OF THE PRAYER SHAWL**	76355-3	$1.75
☐ **THUNDERSTRUCK IN SYRIA**	80860-3	$1.95
☐ **THE MAN WHO SOLD DEATH**	51921-0	$1.75
☐ **THE SUICIDE SEAT**	79077-1	$2.25
☐ **SAFARI OF SPIES**	75330-2	$1.95
☐ **TURKISH BLOODBATH**	82726-8	$2.25
☐ **WAR FROM THE CLOUDS**	87192-5	$2.25
☐ **THE JUDAS SPY**	41295-5	$1.75

 ACE CHARTER BOOKS
P.O. Box 400, Kirkwood, N.Y. 13795   N-01

Please send me the titles checked above. I enclose _____.
Include 75¢ for postage and handling if one book is ordered; 50¢ per book for two to five. If six or more are ordered, postage is free. California, Illinois, New York and Tennessee residents please add sales tax.

NAME_____

ADDRESS_____

CITY_____STATE_____ZIP_____

NICK CARTER